HARNESS AT DALTON SQUARE

LeRoy Neiman

Clydesdales

75TH

1933   2008

ANNIVERSARY

THE GREAT AMERICAN TRADITION

THE 75TH ANNIVERSARY OF THE BUDWEISER CLYDESDALES

BY DIGBY DIEHL

Executive Producers: Bob Fishbeck, Marty Kohr
Art Direction and Design: Gary Alfredson, Larry Butts
Photo Research: Kay Diehl
ISBN - 13: 978-0-9820564-0-0
Printed In The United States by Cenveo, St. Louis

Table of Contents

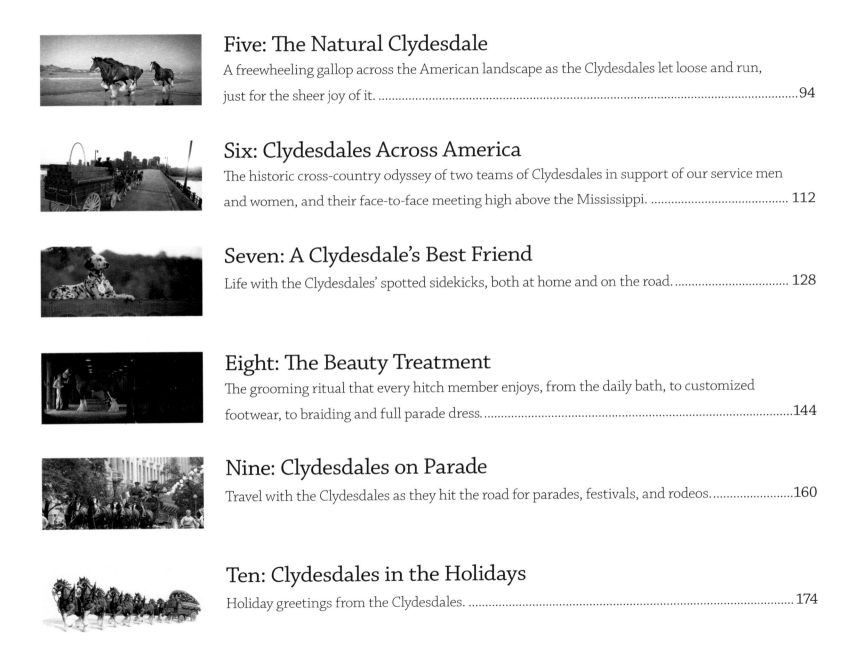

Five: The Natural Clydesdale

A freewheeling gallop across the American landscape as the Clydesdales let loose and run,

Six: Clydesdales Across America

The historic cross-country odyssey of two teams of Clydesdales in support of our service men

Seven: A Clydesdale's Best Friend

Eight: The Beauty Treatment

The grooming ritual that every hitch member enjoys, from the daily bath, to customized

Nine: Clydesdales on Parade

Ten: Clydesdales in the Holidays

"Those Clydesdales are the envy of the equine world. I don't think any horses anywhere are treated with such love, care, and respect.

— Dr. Dallas Goble, DVM, DACVS

“ In 1933, when those first hitches pulled up to the curb on Pestalozzi Street, the drivers, ”
Art Zerr and Billy Wales, climbed down and hugged my father, and the three of them were
crying. I cried too, at the sight of it. It was the most gratifying thing I've ever done in my life.

– August A. "Gussie" Busch, Jr.

“ If the Tournament of Roses parade consisted of just two entries, ”
the Marine Corps band and the Budweiser Clydesdale horses,
I would still get up at 5 o'clock in the morning to see it.

– Zan Thompson, *Los Angeles Times*

Foreword

In 1933, my grandfather, August Busch, Jr.,

presented the first team of Clydesdales to his father,

August Busch, Sr., to commemorate the first bottle

of post-Prohibition Budweiser brewed in St. Louis.

The Clydesdales symbolized a national return to optimism;

Anheuser-Busch was the nation's leading brewer

in the early 1900s, so Americans looked to us

to lead the industry back to prosperity.

For the past 75 years, the Clydesdales have been

an integral part of the American landscape, captivating

crowds at hundreds of celebrations each year.

They symbolize achievement, success, perfection,

and team spirit. Above all, they are a living icon

of Budweiser quality and American integrity.

August A. Busch IV

Introduction

Millions of people have seen the Budweiser Clydesdales

at parades, county fairs, rodeos, or other celebratory events.

Millions more have seen them on television, primarily in the Super Bowl ads.

Talking to individuals about their personal connection with the horses, however,

reveals that the Clydesdales mean many different things to different people.

For some, the Clydesdales are living embodiments of concepts

such as power, beauty, and out-and-out enormity.

For others, they are nostalgic reminders of America's horse-drawn past.

Football fans know them as talented performers in some

of the most innovative and award-winning advertisements of our times.

Beer lovers point to them as Anheuser-Busch's ambassadors of quality and tradition.

And of course, anyone with enough Scottish blood to wear the family kilt

will proudly boast that there is a region bisected by the Clyde River

in rural Lanarkshire where the Clydesdale breed was born.

The Gentle Giants stood out among horses as soon as they were imported into
the United States. In 1849, the great American novelist, Herman Melville,
wrote an admiring description of what certainly seem to be Clydesdales
in his first book, *Redburn: His First Voyage:*

Among all the sights of the docks,
the noble truck-horses are not the least striking to a stranger.
They are large and powerful brutes, with such sleek and glossy coats
that they look as if brushed and put on by a valet every morning.
They march with a slow and stately step,
lifting their ponderous hoofs like royal Siam elephants...
So grave, dignified, gentlemanly, and courteous did these fine truck-horses
look—so full of calm intelligence and sagacity,
that often I endeavored to get into conversation with them,
as they stood in contemplative attitudes while their loads were preparing.
But all I could get from them was the mere recognition of a friendly neigh.

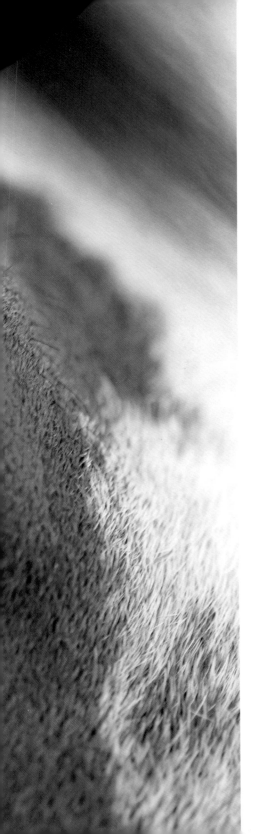

It is marvelous to behold the sense of wonder and the overwhelming feeling

of immensity a person experiences when first seeing a Clydesdale up close.

Yes, it's a horse, but nothing in your life has prepared you for the hugeness that confronts you—

as you look at a Clydesdale, your definition of "big" just got a whole lot bigger.

As you look up at this somewhat familiar figure, you see great, kindly eyes looking down

at you from a large head that is nine feet up in the air.

Everyone is impressed by the stature of these well-trained, friendly giants.

This sweet-natured animal dwarfs even the tallest basketball player.

What fascinated visitors soon discover, however, is that the Budweiser Clydesdales

are celebrities treated to equine amenities beyond the imaginations of recreational horse owners.

Preening a Clydesdale is a full-time job. When they are on the road, a staff of six handlers

spends six hours every day washing and grooming each horse meticulously, parade or no parade.

A staff veterinarian has prescribed the healthiest meals, and the best exercise plans.

To ensure their long-term health, the vet has also placed stringent limits

on the duration of performances and travel times.

The Budweiser Clydesdales were introduced on April 7, 1933

by August A. "Gussie" Busch, Jr. to celebrate the end of Prohibition.

As they paraded smartly down Pestalozzi Street to the front of the brewery in St. Louis, they

were an immediate symbol of pride, quality, and tradition to the surprised and delighted crowd.

No one was more delighted, however, than Gussie's father, August A., Sr.,

who wept with joy at the sight of them.

From that day forward, they have continued to please and amaze crowds of fans across the country.

Today there are five Clydesdale hitches that crisscross America, visiting approximately five hundred

cities and towns each year. Those lucky five hundred venues are only one-half of the requests

for appearances that Anheuser-Busch receives each year.

One of the most important contributions of the Budweiser Clydesdales to American life

was the "Clydesdales Across America" event of 2005.

This salute to American heroes honored our military forces, as well as police, fire, and medical

assistance personnel whose daily jobs ensure our safety and freedom,

both as a nation and as individuals.

One hitch began in San Francisco, the other in New York, stopping in cities

and small towns en route to an historic rendezvous over the Mississippi River.

At each stop, thousands of Americans videotaped messages of encouragement

and support to our service men and women overseas.

When the hitches met on the Eads Bridge in St. Louis on the Fourth of July,

the symbolic union was celebrated with a huge fireworks display.

The chapters that follow chronicle every aspect of the lives of these fabulous horses. From their inception at the end of Prohibition, you will see the important role the Clydesdales have played in American history. You will go behind the scenes to see the pre- and post-performance rituals of the Clydesdales and their handlers—how they are stabled, how they travel, how they are groomed, fed, and exercised. We will also take you to the Budweiser Breeding and Training Ranches, where you will follow a newborn colt from its youngest years, through various training experiences and into a new role as a member of the hitch. Along the way we will introduce you to some of the men and women who believe they have the best jobs in America—the people who train, care for, and drive the Clydesdale hitches. We will show you the Dalmatians who are their pals. Best of all, we will invite you to ride along on some of the most memorable performances of the Clydesdales in the past 75 years...so enjoy this anniversary celebration of the Budweiser Clydesdales and their 75 years of celebrating American tradition.

CHAPTER 1

75 Years of Making Friends

In 1857, an entrepreneurial 18-year-old German immigrant named Adolphus Busch arrived in St. Louis via New Orleans. The youngest of 21 children, Adolphus had been well-educated in his native Mainz, but followed his brothers to the United States to make his fortune. After a few years as a "mud clerk" on the banks of the Mississippi, he used his inheritance to go into the brewery supply business. One of his customers was Eberhard Anheuser, owner of the struggling E. Anheuser & Co. Brewery. A prosperous soap manufacturer, in 1860 Anheuser had taken possession of what had been known as the Bavarian Brewery (founded by Georg Schneider in 1852) as payment for an outstanding debt.

Anheuser was inexperienced in the making of beer, and began seeking the counsel of his brewery supplier on how to improve his business. Soon Adolphus Busch began making social calls on the Anheuser household, and before long he became one of the family. In 1861, Adolphus Busch married one of Anheuser's daughters, Lilly. Adolphus' brother Ulrich married Lilly's sister Anna on the same day. As Adolphus advised his father-in-law on how to upgrade his product, sales and profits began to climb.

In the late 1860s, Adolphus began to devote an increasing amount of his time to his father-in-law's brewery. He became a full partner in 1869, the same year that the Golden Spike was driven in Promontory, Utah, uniting the Union Pacific and Central Pacific railroads and making coast-to-coast rail travel possible. Already aware of how railroads were changing commerce in Europe, Adolphus immediately grasped the importance of transcontinental rail transport for the brewery—it would now be feasible to market beer all across America.

After a trip to Europe where he became acquainted with the work of Louis Pasteur, he became the first U.S. brewer to introduce pasteurization to the brewing process. Now sure that his beer was stable enough to travel well, Busch acquired a fleet of refrigerated railway cars and established the St. Louis Refrigerator Car Company to transport his new flagship national product: Budweiser. Introduced in 1876, it was an immediate success, and the first national beer brand in the United States. Just two years later, Budweiser was marketed overseas, and could be found in Cape Town, Hong Kong, Rio de Janeiro, and London.

Budweiser was doing well overseas, but distribution within the United States was crucial. The country's expanding web of railways efficiently moved large shipments of the heavy and cumbersome barrels and cases out of St. Louis, but they still had to be delivered to their final destinations. And for that, strong horses were essential. From the earliest years, Anheuser-Busch products were delivered by horse-drawn wagons, often to small towns and remote areas of the western frontier.

According to legend,
in the days when horses
pulled the beer wagons,
a brewer's success
was measured
by how far his draft
horses could pull
their load
in a day's time.
Although these early
Anheuser-Busch horses
were strong,
they were not
Clydesdales.
The first Clydesdales
were imported
into Canada
from Scotland in 1842.
Although a few
were brought
into the United States
from Canada
in the years that followed,
it was not until the 1880s
that they were imported
in large numbers.
By 1910 there were
16,000 of them in the U.S.

Serving trays were among the most popular promotional giveaways. Adolphus Busch gave out corkscrew knives to clients in lieu of business cards, and they are still collectors' items today. Many had a photo of Adolphus visible through a peephole Stanhope lens on the handle.

From his early days as a salesman on the Mississippi, Adolphus Busch was always looking for innovative ways to market his product. There was perhaps more than a little P. T. Barnum in Adolphus—to boost the sales of Budweiser, he pioneered consumer promotional giveaways (the pocket knife/corkscrew was especially popular) as well as the use of attractive women in beer advertising.

And it worked—so well that by the turn of the century, Anheuser-Busch was producing a million barrels of beer a year.

The success of the brewery made Adolphus and his wife, Lilly, two of St. Louis' most prominent and prosperous citizens. Ever magnanimous, they generously supported civic causes, especially relating to orphans and crippled children, and opened their home every Saturday to folks in need. On other days of the week they entertained artists, royalty, and captains of industry at their opulent Victorian mansion at No. 1 Busch Place.

W hen Adolphus and Lilly entertained, the
carriages of their guests were sheltered at the family stable nearby,
and there was nothing modest about it. A lifelong animal lover,
Adolphus was adamant that his horses, those of his guests, and

The
Magnificent New
PRIVATE STABLE
of
Adolphus Busch.
Esq.

An Equine Palace
All Horse lovers should visit.

those delivering beer from the brewery were well treated. He was
equally concerned about the safety and well-being of his employees.
Every inch a patriarch, Adolphus Busch considered brewery workers
to be members of his extended family. Cared for by the company,
employees were expected to be loyal in return.

The luxurious Busch family stable was an "equine palace."
Constructed in 1885 at a cost of $35,000, the huge stable was
patterned after a railroad roundhouse. It housed thirty-five of
Adolphus' own horses and a variety of elegant conveyances–landaus,
barouches, depot wagons, and phaetons.

As the 20th century dawned, Anheuser-Busch continued to grow and prosper, but the temperance movement gained strength and political clout. Although temperance advocates had begun with good intentions, preaching only moderation, by the turn of the century they started pressing more stridently–and more belligerently–for complete abstinence. While Carrie Nation garnered headlines by bursting into taverns and smashing bottles with a hatchet, Wayne Wheeler's Anti-Saloon League worked behind the scenes, using money and political muscle to make and break candidates of both parties on the issue of prohibition alone.

Yoked to the women's suffrage movement, prohibition was touted as the key to a better society and a better quality of life for women in particular, bringing an end to poverty, crime, and domestic violence that sprang from alcohol abuse. Wheeler and others, however, also whipped up anti-German sentiment during World War I to turn public opinion against the brewers, who were largely of German descent. The 18th Amendment to the Constitution was ratified on January 29, 1919; the Volstead Act, providing enforcement for the amendment, was passed on October 28 of the same year. The United States officially went dry on January 16, 1920.

Many brewers were caught flatfooted. Believing the temperance movement to be little more than a nuisance, they had refused to imagine that America would ever embrace complete abstinence. Adolphus Busch, however, had seen the danger as early as 1889, and had begun exploring ways to diversify beyond beer into the manufacture of other products. In 1906, Adolphus directed the brewery's brewmaster to begin work on a nonalcoholic cereal drink. The product was still in development in 1913 when Adolphus passed away, but his son, August A. Busch, continued working to improve the new nonalcoholic beverage.

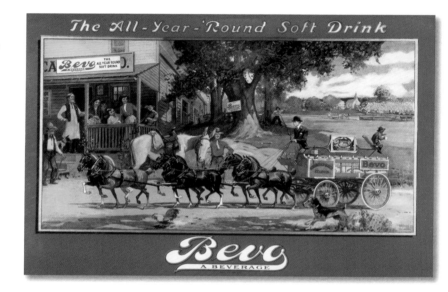

The Bevo Pony hitch was part of what was becoming an Anheuser-Busch marketing trademark— the use of animals in product promotion.

The result was Bevo. Made from barley malt, rice, hops, and yeast, it was introduced for sale in 1916. The company put a big marketing push behind it, advertising Bevo on billboards, in magazines, and with a number of promotional gimmicks.

Bevo was a huge success, at least at first. By 1918, Anheuser-Busch was selling more than 5 million cases a year, and built a new $10 million bottling plant (then and now the largest under one roof) in an attempt to keep up with demand.

A hitch of Shetland ponies, bred at Grant's Farm (first owned by President Ulysses S. Grant and later acquired by August A. Busch, Sr.) and pulling a miniature wagon, made the rounds of county fairs.

With the advent of Prohibition, August A. Busch and others in brewery management were dumbfounded when demand for Bevo precipitously tanked. By 1921, sales had dropped to just 400,000 cases—less than 10 percent of the peak three years earlier. The problem was that Americans were thumbing their noses at Prohibition, finding

In World War I, the Anheuser-Busch vehicle department developed a special land cruiser for use by the Army as a reconnaissance vehicle. The boatcar could travel on both land and water, but the war ended before it could be put into production. Anheuser-Busch used the boatcar to promote Bevo and sent it touring around the country.

black market means to procure alcohol, or making their own. As a result, Bevo was no longer in competition with other nonalcoholic beverages, but with home brew and a host of illegal spirits. Bevo sales continued to plummet throughout the 1920s, and the product was finally discontinued in 1929.

s Bevo sales nosedived, the company scrambled to develop new products to sell. Any resources and ingredients traditionally used in beer were pressed into service and adapted to other uses. "Essentially," said August A. Busch, Sr. at the time, "our business has always been the conversion of grain into other products." A parade of soft drinks, including Kaffo (coffee flavored), Carcho (chocolate flavored), Buschtee (tea flavored), Grape Bouquet, and root beer, was launched. None found favor with the public.

The company also tapped into its other areas of expertise, especially its ability to make and ship products requiring refrigeration. Ice cream was manufactured in the New Orleans branch, and by 1926, sales exceeded a million gallons annually. They focused on the making of refrigerated truck bodies to move dairy products and other perishables, and later segued into the manufacture of refrigerated cabinets for commercial establishments.

BIG TOM AT REST

A TRAVELING HOTEL FOR TOM THE GIANT OX

Big Tom, the largest ox in the world, was a marketing star for barley malt syrup, and toured the country pulling his own deluxe accommodations (his "traveling hotel") behind him. The standing figure at right in the straw boater hat is August A. Busch, Sr. Like the Bevo hitch of Shetland ponies, Tom was one of several early Anheuser-Busch efforts to use animals in promotional campaigns.

Prohibition did not create the Depression, but it certainly aggravated it once it got started. Brewery cities such as St. Louis and Cincinnati were particularly hard hit, and the ripples of poverty and despair extended far beyond the brewery employees themselves. Anheuser-Busch had to liquidate some of its real estate holdings and do some in-house belt-tightening, but it was in the black three years after Prohibition began. Due to the foresight of company leadership, unlike most breweries it was able to retain more than half its workforce. Because of the close and supportive relationship Anheuser-Busch had cultivated with its employees, this was a point of pride.

The company also made a premium extra dry ginger ale, which struggled for

AMERICA'S FINEST GINGER ALE

profitability because it was "too good." Although product advertising stressed its exclusivity and highbrow sophistication, it had trouble competing with lesser mixers, which were able to undercut the price.

Throughout Prohibition, the market was flooded with cheap ginger ale, which consumers used to take the edge off the harsh taste of bad bootleg booze.

One surprise revenue generator was barley malt syrup, which was at first marketed only to commercial bakers and pharmaceutical companies. Soon, however, it was being purchased in surprising quantity by the general public, but people weren't using it to bake bread or cookies. Barley malt syrup was a key ingredient in tasty home-brewed beer.

As the miseries of the Depression mounted, so did popular sentiment for the repeal of a clearly failing Prohibition. Far from ending poverty and violence, it had exacerbated it. Battling crime syndicates warred openly in the streets for the right to supply America's major cities with alcohol, and all over the country people were dying from wood alcohol sold by unscrupulous bootleggers. Prohibition not only fattened the coffers of gangsters and racketeers, it made criminals and victims of otherwise law-abiding citizens.

In 1932, Franklin Roosevelt campaigned for the presidency on a pledge to end Prohibition, and called Congress into special session soon after taking office to pass repeal legislation. On March 23, 1933, Anheuser-Busch received permission from the state of Missouri to resume brewing, and immediately began rehiring some 1,700 workers to gear up for production. Anheuser-Busch had survived Prohibition and was back in the beer business. Other breweries had not fared nearly as well. Of the 1,568 breweries in the country in 1910, only 714 reopened when Prohibition ended.

The rest had gone under, victims of the so-called "noble experiment."

Although hard liquor was still illegal until the final ratification of the 21st Amendment in December, the prohibition on beer in Missouri and several other states ended as of April 7, 1933. An exuberant crowd estimated at 25,000 people assembled in the streets around the Bevo plant as the clock ticked down.

Anheuser-Busch brought out a brass band to celebrate, and August A. Busch, Jr. (known affectionately in the press as "Gussie") delivered an 11 minute broadcast on national radio in honor of the occasion. "Once again," he intoned in his trademark gravel voice, "freight cars are pulling in, loaded with grain from American farms…while others will soon be rolling out and onward, contributing their share toward the rehabilitation of industry, agriculture and transportation." When the clock struck 12, he declared that "Happy Days Are Here Again" (FDR's theme song), and announced that free beer was being served to the enthusiastic throng gathered at the brewery.

J ust a few days earlier, Gussie had entered the office of his ailing father. "I told him I wanted to show him a new car I just bought," he recalled. August A. Busch, Sr. scowled his disapproval at the profligate purchase—although Prohibition was ending, the country was still mired in the Great Depression, and times were uncertain. Nevertheless he agreed to accompany his

son downstairs. Gussie Busch had taken a page of razzle-dazzle from his grandfather Adolphus. At a prearranged signal, Gussie's "car" came into view, except it wasn't a car at all. Instead, two six-horse hitches of champion Clydesdales, driven by Art Zerr and Billy Wales and each hauling a spiffy red vintage beer wagon, smartly heather-stepped down Pestalozzi Street to the brewery entrance. August A. Busch, Sr. was so overjoyed that he was moved to tears. "Art and Billy climbed down and hugged my father," Gussie continued, "and the three of them were crying. I cried too, at the sight of it. It was the most gratifying thing I've ever done in my life."

Taken in March of 1933, this is the earliest known photograph of the Budweiser Clydesdale hitch. In the driver's seat is Billy Wales, the "Magician of the Ribbons [reins]." Something of a celebrity in his own right, Wales had toured with Buffalo Bill. At one point his hands were insured for $50,000.

T hroughout his career, Gussie Busch was known both for his flamboyant showmanship and for his highly innovative – and highly successful–approach to marketing. After the surprise presentation, Gussie sent the Zerr hitch to Chicago as the first stop on a midwestern tour, and put the Wales hitch on an eastbound train. Wales and his New York-bound champion horses were tasked with

making a very important special delivery. After picking up a case of beer that had been specially flown by chartered aircraft to Newark Airport, the Clydesdales rumbled through the Holland Tunnel and up Fifth Avenue to the front of the gleaming new Empire State Building (less than two years old at the time) to make a ceremonial presentation. The grateful recipient was former New York governor Al Smith, long a foe of Prohibition.

After appearances in New York City, Billy Wales and the six-horse hitch were again transported by rail, this time to Washington, D.C. There, they delivered another one of the special first cases of beer to President Franklin D. Roosevelt.

The "Certificate of Priority" was presented with each of the first cases of Budweiser to be brewed in the initial post-Prohibition batch. Although there were several hundred such certificates presented with cases to "friends of Budweiser," they have become rarities and are now considered collector's items. They reflect, with great sincerity, the relief felt by August Busch that the brewery was back to doing what they had been doing since 1876: making a fine quality lager enjoyed by millions of people ~ Budweiser.

After these first ceremonial deliveries, Wales and Zerr then took their hitches on tour. All travel from city to city was by railroad car. As they toured the country, promoting the return of beer to a thirsty nation, Gussie's gift to his father turned into an immediate public relations and marketing sensation.

Prohibition was directly responsible. When Prohibition began, horses were still commonly found on the streets of every city in America. Although many delivery companies had started phasing in trucks, in 1920 a hitch of powerful horses pulling a beer wagon would not have been particularly unusual. The thirteen dry years, however, were just long enough to complete the

triumph of the internal combustion engine. By the time the hitches hit the road in 1933, the Clydesdales were a novelty, a nostalgic reminder of a gentler, more prosperous time, and a sight many had never seen before. It is a novelty that continues into the 21st century.

Where did the Budweiser Clydesdales come from? Late in 1932, Gussie Busch had attended the International Livestock Exhibition in Chicago with his father, and had noted his father's delight at seeing the six-horse hitch classes perform. Particularly taken with the Clydesdales, in December of 1932 he secretly approached the Anheuser-Busch Board of Directors for permission to purchase a hitch. After receiving the okay, in February he was able to purchase two champion six-horse hitches, one from the Chicago Union Stockyards, and a second from the Wilson Meat Packing Company, for a total of $21,000. The Board of Directors and everyone else who knew of the acquisition kept Gussie's secret until he presented the horses to his father, just as Prohibition was ending. That May he bought a third hitch from the Shea Brewing Company of Winnipeg, Manitoba, providing additional relief animals and enabling the hitches to grow from six to eight horses.

The Clydesdales attracted attention wherever they went, and the hitches were a high-profile component of the Anheuser-Busch promotional campaign celebrating the return of bottled beer. These national tours continued through the 1930s and early 1940s. The horses traveled by private railroad car until 1941 when they got their own Clydesdale Caravan.

Now billed as the World Famous Budweiser Clydesdales, from this point forward they were to travel in style in specially appointed vans. The dedication of the new vans was celebrated with great fanfare on May 16, 1941. Both Gussie Busch and Adolphus Busch, III attended.

The new vans were in use for less than a year before the war put the Clydesdales out of circulation. America's entry into World War II after Pearl Harbor brought gas rationing to the nation. As part of the war effort, early in 1943, Anheuser-Busch voluntarily ceased selling Budweiser on the west coast. The freight cars that would have carried the beer westward were instead devoted to moving military supplies, and the Clydesdales remained stabled in St. Louis until V-J Day in 1945.

After World War II ended, the Clydesdales toured the country, as they had before the war. Although they still made the rounds of small towns and county fairs, the Clydesdales increasingly began performing before larger audiences. In March of 1949, they were the stars of Pennsylvania Avenue. Missouri native Harry Truman invited them to perform in his inaugural parade. It was the Clydesdales' first presidential command performance, but not their last—some 44 years later, they marched in the 1993 Clinton inaugural.

President Truman got a closer look at the Clydesdales when he visited Grant's Farm in June of 1950. An avid horseman like his father and grandfather before him, Gussie Busch took Truman for a ride around the grounds, driving the carriage himself—although the horses in the picture above are not Clydesdales.

This 1983 photograph of the hitch coming through the Grant's Farm gate replicates the opening sequence of The Ken Murray Show.

At the dawn of a new decade, the Clydesdales joined the television age, still in its infancy, parading through the iron gates of Grant's Farm in the opening credits of *The Ken Murray Show*. Anheuser-Busch was a sponsor of the one-hour hit CBS Saturday night variety program, which debuted on April 15, 1950. At about the same time, the Clydesdales gained a spotted sidekick as the Dalmatians made their debut with the hitch.

By the 1950s, despite the burgeoning popularity of the Clydesdale hitches, the breed itself was in trouble. Because no one used them on the farm anymore, the only remaining Clydesdales

In 1952, Gussie Busch took the reins of the hitch in New York's Times Square for the dedication of the large, highly visible Anheuser-Busch neon sign.

were show horses. Not surprisingly, their numbers were dwindling rapidly and the breed was in danger of dying out. Gussie Busch was both sentimental about the Clydesdales and cognizant of their promotional power. In 1953 he again purchased a group of Scottish Clydesdales. Crossing the Atlantic on the S.S. Egidia, they were brought to Grant's Farm to initiate a breeding program. This acquisition has been credited with saving the breed in North America.

The year 1953 marked the Clydesdales' first participation in the Tournament of Roses in Pasadena, pulling the City of St. Louis prize-winning float. They have pulled the St. Louis entry every year since, and remain the only nonmotorized float in the parade.

That year also marked another important event in Anheuser-Busch history, as Gussie Busch persuaded the Anheuser-Busch board of directors to acquire the St. Louis Cardinals baseball team, which was on the brink of relocating out of town. (Total price: $3.75 million) "My ambition is, whether hell or high water, to get a championship baseball team for St. Louis before I die," he declared. It took some years for the team to be successful, and there were years when it appeared that hell or high water might show up first, but eventually the Cardinals became a National League powerhouse. If the team made the playoffs, Mr. Busch, a lifelong baseball fan,

Long before 1953, the Busch family had established a close connection with the city of Pasadena. Adolphus and Lilly Busch had maintained a large winter home there, and a second next door for their children. In 1913, Adolphus Busch had entered this elaborate rose-covered carriage into the parade.

would often ride into Busch Stadium on the Clydesdale wagon, waving his trademark red cowboy hat.

In 1967, the Clydesdales hit Broadway in their first Macy's Thanksgiving Day Parade. They had already taken Manhattan in June of that year, however, in their first appearance in the annual Puerto Rican Day Parade. As they traveled down Fifth Avenue, they carried an added passenger–Johnny Carson's late night sidekick Ed McMahon, who had been the Budweiser celebrity spokesman since 1963. (Carson jokingly referred to McMahon as "Clydesdale breath" on air.) Throughout much of the 1960s and 1970s, McMahon was the voice of the Budweiser promotional spots. He often appeared on camera with the Clydesdales, including one commercial in 1978, when for the first (and only) time, a Clydesdale "talked" on television. Year by year, these commercials increased in prestige and quality.

This 1953 flower-covered riverboat is the first St. Louis entry in the Rose Parade, and the first appearance of the Clydesdales in the parade.

The 1970s were noteworthy for one holiday tradition which continues today—the Clydesdale TV Holiday spot. The decade also saw the first major expansion of the Clydesdale program. Shortly after a new brewery was constructed in Merrimack, New Hampshire in 1970, a Clydesdale facility was added. With a design modeled on the historic Bauernhof building at Grant's Farm, the Merrimack Clydesdale Hamlet opened in 1972 and became the home of the East Coast hitch. Demand for Clydesdale appearances, however, continued to increase. By 1975, the horses were logging more than 40,000 miles annually; nevertheless, Clydesdale Operations was forced to turn down many invitations each year. By this time, however, there was another location for the Clydesdales. A new brewery and Busch Gardens entertainment complex at Williamsburg, Virginia featured some of the Budweiser Clydesdales.

As the 1970s ended, the Clydesdale program grew yet again. In the 1980s, a second breeding facility was established at the 900-acre Warm Springs Ranch in Menifee, California, about sixty miles southeast of Los Angeles. This location also became the home base for the new West Coast hitch. When a new brewery was planned for Ft. Collins, Colorado, another Clydesdale breeding and training facility was incorporated into the design. In the 1980s, the Clydesdales became goodwill ambassadors, traveling by air to Alaska and to Japan.

During this period, there was also a hitch stationed at Santa Anita Race Track in Arcadia, California, which pulled the starting gate into position before each race. (The photograph on this page was taken during a performance at Churchill Downs, Louisville, Kentucky.)

The year 1983 was marked with great fanfare—it was the Clydesdales' 50th anniversary. For the occasion, special horseshoes were made with the 50th anniversary logo on them, and on April 7, 1983, August Busch III made a ceremonial presentation to his father, August Busch, Jr., the man who had surprised his

father with the hitches a half century earlier. The Clydesdales were present, of course, for the cutting of the 50th anniversary cake. The commemorative ceremony took place near the corner of Ninth and Pestalozzi Streets, at virtually the same spot where the Clydesdales had made their debut 50 years earlier.

By this time, the numbers that the Clydesdales had stacked up were staggering. They had covered almost 1.3 million miles in 50 years, marching in over 3,000 parades and appearing at nearly 7,000 events. In the process, they had gone through almost 13,000 pounds of show harness, and over 300,000 paper flowers for their manes. They'd also worn out more than 35,000 horseshoes.

Pictured on the left are August Busch III and August Busch, Jr. cutting the 50th anniversary cake. Above is a souvenir 50th anniversary Clydesdale horseshoe. In the photograph on the right August "Gussie" Busch, Jr. takes a ride on the hitch, and waves to the 50th anniversary crowd with his traditional red hat.

38

The familiar strains of "Here Comes The King" floated down Pestalozzi Street as a crowd of six thousand people lined the avenue on April 7, 2008. They saw the red and leopard clad Mystic Sheiks of Morocco brass band from Busch Gardens, Tampa lead a Budweiser Clydesdale hitch in a re-creation of their first appearance 75 years ago, the day that Prohibition ended. The brewery shut down at noon, and members of the entire Anheuser-Busch family from all over the country gathered to raise a glass of icy cold Bud in celebration.

Anheuser-Busch executives greeted employees as they joined the festivities, including David A. Peacock, Vice-President of Marketing; Tom Shipley, Director of Budweiser Marketing, and Bob Fishbeck, Budweiser Product Manager. Matt and Chris, two of the most famous Clydesdales from the Super Bowl commercials, also were on hand to welcome the crowd, as were a yellow and white python and a friendly armadillo from Busch Gardens.

In the shadow of the Bevo fox, on a platform in front of the historic Bevo Building, dignitaries lauded the company and the Clydesdales for their long tradition of quality, as the hitch stood proudly by to the delight of onlookers. St. Louis Mayor Francis Slay and Missouri Lieutenant Governor Peter Kinder praised the economic contributions of the company to the city and the state. August A. Busch IV, President and CEO of Anheuser-Busch, addressed the cheering crowd, gave away a new Harley-Davidson and gave full credit for the success of the company " to the best employees of any company anywhere in the world."

41

CHAPTER 2

Stars of the Media

Clydesdale Football
(1995)

In 1995, America was introduced to a whole new way of looking at the Clydesdales. Unbridled, unbraided, unhitched, and

unharnessed, the Clydesdales became the stars of a memorable series of Super Bowl promotional spots that captured the imagination

and tickled the funny bone of the country. Although the Clydesdales had always been popular, in these ads they let their hair down

Ad Agency: DDB Chicago; Creative Team: Craig Feigen, Adam Glickman, Greg Popp; Director: Anthony Hoffman; Director of Photography: Conrad Hall

and became hip—without losing their dignity. Year after year, these commercials remain among the highest rated and most fondly remembered by men and women of all ages. Bob Lachky, Executive Vice President-Global Industry Development and Creative Development, focused on the Budweiser Clydesdales as representatives of Anheuser-Busch and performers of enjoyable anthropomorphic antics.

It all started with Clydesdale Football, which was the brainchild of Adam Glickman and Craig Feigen of the ad agency DDB Chicago, who were tasked with finding something fresh. "We asked ourselves what we could do with the Clydesdales that had never been done before," recalls Feigen. "Everyone loved the idea of the Clydesdales playing football, but it was shelved because it was so wild that no one was really sure it could be done."

"One company wanted to do it with computer generation," adds Glickman, "but we knew we couldn't make it look contrived or hokey. We had to show the Clydesdales running as real horses in all their grandeur."

Media animal trainer Robin Wiltshire–well known for his sensitivity with animals–was asked to prepare the Clydesdales for their High Chaparral gridiron debut. "We chose Robin to train them to work as naturally as possible," says Feigen.

Not many inquiries faze Robin Wiltshire, but even he was surprised by a telephone call from a production company in Los Angeles. "I want to train Clydesdales to play football," declared the young woman on the other end of the line.

He had less than a month to do it. "That's not much time, so I have to completely dedicate myself to those horses. I have to get into the mind of each horse. When I'm training or working on set, I don't let too many other people talk to them, because I need them to be beamed in on my voice." Born in Australia, Wiltshire moved to Wyoming in the 1980s, but retains his distinctive Down Under speech pattern. His trademark Stetson is a part of his daily uniform.

How does he get such amazing performances out of his four-legged actors? "It's all about making the trick easy to understand for the animal," he explains. With a total of 26 Clydesdales (11 horses and two understudies for each team in the "game"), every step in the process had to be taught incrementally, one small piece at a time, as the Clydesdales learned. "You start them off one by one, just you and the horse," Wiltshire continues. "You teach him to go left or right when you point. You teach 'come to me,' and 'stop' until each horse can do it out in the open, by himself. Then you put two horses together and have them do it, then three. Then you try the same three together every day, for a couple of days."

Wiltshire trained each team to come right up to a slender line of masking tape, and then stop. "I had to get them to know which side they were on," says Wiltshire. "That was crucial. Before we could go any further, they had to know exactly who their buddies were." Some pairs and trios buddied up better than others, so it was a process of mix and match to sort out the opposing teams. Eventually Wiltshire had two complete 11-horse teams of Clydesdales, each trained to work as a unit. "I had a red team and a blue team. The red team stayed together and the blue team stayed together."

The Clydesdales trained at Wiltshire's Turtle Ranch near Jackson Hole, Wyoming, before heading for tiny Stanley, Idaho, to shoot. "I think the film crew pretty much doubled the population when we arrived," quips former DDB executive Dennis Ryan. "We used Stanley because the Sawtooth Mountains in the background are at 8,000 feet rather than 14,000 feet, and they fit in the viewfinder."

As Wiltshire continued working with the Clydesdales, a few "stars" emerged. A bit more intelligent and quicker to learn their roles than their brethren, Marty, Matt, and Chris distinguished themselves and were trained to rear, to hold the ball, and to kick it.

Marty reared. Chris was the holder—and trained first with a block of wood. West Coast hitch member Matt, who resides at Warm Springs Ranch in Menifee, California, was the kicker. He was one of the younger horses. "I was visiting Menifee," Wiltshire recalls, "and it had been years since I'd seen Matt. When I whistled out to him, he immediately kicked his leg straight out in front of him, like I'd taught him to do. It was automatic—after all those years, he still remembered his cue."

Since that time, Matt, Marty, and Chris have appeared in several more commercials. "I have a great time with the Clydesdales—some of them have unbelievable personalities. You bond with them, and they get so close to you in such a short time," Wiltshire says.

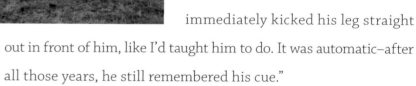

Robin Wiltshire teaches a Clydesdale to rear on command,
using the same techniques of positive reinforcement that are used in all of their training.
The whip is used only for the sound it makes in mid-air, and never touches the horse.

Clydesdale Dream
(1998)

Everyone can identify with the baby Clydesdale running along the fence to catch up with the hitch, hoping one day to join it, because he echoes our common human quest for greater things. When the lead horse turns back to wink at him, it's one of advertising's best remembered gifts from a hero to a starstruck youngster. It is the embodiment of every child's American Dream.

"The little foal in the meadow was named Sonny, and he was just seven months old when we shot this," recalls Robin Wiltshire.

Ad Agency: DDB Chicago; Creative Team: Craig Feigen, Adam Glickman, Don Pogany, Greg Popp; Director: Geoffry Barish

"I had to train him to lie down on the ground, then lift his head, look around, and finally get up. He had to do that take about a dozen times, because they wanted to get the light just right. Here was this little horse–he'd never been on set before and he just took it all for granted.

"The most difficult part of *Clydesdale Dream* was actually at the end, where the lead horse looks back and winks. In the shot, that horse was actually walking as he turned his head back, which is quite hard for a horse to do, because his balance is not there."

"This referee is a jackass." "Nope, I believe that's a zebra." For anyone who's ever questioned the eyesight or IQ of a referee, this one's for you. Like many in the stands and watching at home, the Clydesdales on the field snort their impatience while the official clad in black and white reviews the play on the sidelines. The referee in *Replay* is a 30-year-old zebra senior citizen named Ty.

Ad Agency: Hill Holliday; Creative Team: Eivind Ueland, Doug Gould; Director: Zack Snyder

Obviously, the football game has been stopped for a crucial ruling on a challenged play. Wiltshire enticed Ty to stick his head into the curtained instant replay reviewing box with a pail of grain pellets. When this ad ran during Super Bowl 2003, it was the top rated spot. This was the fifth consecutive year that Anheuser-Busch was at the top of *USA Today's* ranking of Super Bowl commercials, a string that is ongoing.

A Clydesdale trapped in a donkey's body auditions for the hitch. When the large horses inquire, "What makes you think you can be a Clydesdale, son?" the decibel level in the barn goes up alarmingly with a loud bray. Later, as we see the donkey with the hitch, she says, "I must have said something right."

"The donkey in this spot is a gifted actress named Lucille, and she is an amazing little performer," says Robin Wiltshire. "The main thing in the training was getting her to come in close enough to the Clydesdales, and then teaching her to stay in one place, so she didn't get trodden on. She only came up to their knees. That poor little donkey could easily have walked underneath those Clydesdales.

"She was not afraid of them, which I think resulted from her being brought up next door to Grant's Farm in St. Louis. She probably got to see a lot of those big Clydesdales right next to her—not in the same pasture, but chewing grass across the fence.

"We were so lucky to find her. She walked into the stables for the 'interview' with the Clydesdales lined up, and she'd actually already done everything that we shot. When the director asked for a reshoot, I wasn't sure she would sound off again, but then she put this little bray on, and she did three or four takes like that. I did have two of the horses trained to lower their heads at my signal, but when Lucille started braying, it was nothing like anything they'd ever heard before, so they did it for real, which is so much better."

Lucille boosted the popularity of the donkeys in residence at the SeaWorld and Busch Gardens entertainment centers, and if you look carefully, you'll see their hair extensions hanging near the stable door. Putting a donkey together with the Clydesdales, however, is actually nothing new. Before the Second World War, a donkey billed as "the smallest in the world" traveled with the hitches around the country.

Ad Agency: Goodby, Silverstein & Partners; Creative Team: Steve Dildarian, Tyler Magnusson, Jeff Goodby; Director: Jeff Goodby; Producer: James Horner

Snowball Fight
(2005)

When the youngsters decide to have some fun at the expense of their elders, they end up paying the price as a treeful of snow is dumped upon them. "The youngsters in *Snowball Fight* had never seen snow," explains Robin Wiltshire. "In the beginning they were a little afraid of it–these were California horses and they'd never seen the stuff before. I brought in two dump trucks full of snow, and at first I had to lead them up to it. They'd paw at it and sniff it, and then shy away. Two days later they were rolling in it."

Ad Agency: DDB Chicago; Creative Team: Mark Gross, Chris Roe, Chuck Rachford; Producer: Marianne Newton; Director: Baker Smith

"The 'snowballs' were actually white basketballs," Wiltshire continues. "I trained the young horses to roll the balls and then hike them with their feet. These little guys had never been off the ranch before. You wouldn't think they'd present themselves, but as soon as I said 'action,' they were on! They'd just come alive, like it was bred into them." To the viewer's eye, the snowballs looked real. So did the snow falling from the tree, although it actually fell from a bin high above camera range.

Clydesdale American Dream
(2006)

This 2006 warmhearted commercial is among the most fondly remembered promotional spots of all, and earned noted director Joe Pytka a nomination from the Directors Guild of America for Outstanding Directorial Achievement in Commercials. The star of the spot is Evan, the Little Clydesdale Who Could (with a little clandestine help from his grown-up friends). The tag line, "I won't tell if you won't," gives

Ad Agency: DDB Chicago; Creative Team: Steve Bougdanos, Patrick Knoll, Barry Burdiak, John Hayes; Producer: Kate Hildebrant; Director: Joe Pytka

viewers an active role, letting us in on the secret. Of course, the ad is a wonderful parable about striving to be the best–and about how a little encouragement can make all the difference. Evan is now a three-year-old trainee, just beginning to learn his role as a member of the West Coast hitch. *Clydesdale American Dream* is one of those inspirational classics that will live in our memories forever.

Clydesdale Team
(2008)

With the line, "The Patriots' streak was broken, but Anheuser-Busch's was not," *USA Today* announced that for the tenth consecutive year, A-B had the top Super Bowl commercial in 2008, as rated by *USA Today's* Ad Meter real-time consumer poll. *Clydesdale Team*, created by the DDB Chicago agency team, shows the combination of heart and hard work it takes to make the Budweiser Clydesdale hitch.

Ad Agency: DDB Chicago; Creative Team: Steve Bougdanos, Patrick Knoll, Barry Burdiak, John Hayes; Producer: Kate Hildebrant; Director: Joe Pytka

When Hank the Clydesdale is told, "Maybe next year..." he is one depressed horse. But to the strains of the familiar *Rocky* theme music, his Dalmatian personal trainer puts Hank to work. After running along country roads and pulling railroad cars along the tracks by himself, he tries out for the hitch a year later. This time, he is greeted with a "Welcome aboard, Hank"–and a high-five from his trainer!

The Ad Meter-winning Budweiser Clydesdale commercial, *Clydesdale Team*, at Super Bowl 2008 was once again the invention of the DDB creative team, director Joe Pytka, and the remarkably talented horse trainer, Robin Wiltshire. "We actually used three different Clydesdales to play the role of Hank in the commercial," notes Wiltshire. "Chris, one of my favorite stars, did the running and the high-five; Parker pulled the 22 ton rail car; and Joey did the weaving in-and-out of the aspens in the snow."

Filmed in Thousand Oaks and Fillmore in California, the commercial was definitely a product of Pytka's famed attention to detail. "We trained several Clydesdales to perform different hi-fives with one of my dogs," says Wiltshire. (The Dalmatian in the spot is played by two Anheuser-Busch hitch dogs, Cowboy and Andy, who were trained by Robin's wife, Kate.) "But we decided to 'green screen' the shot rather than risk the damage that an accident with a 2,000 pound horse might do to a 70 pound dog." Many scenes in the original script by Craig Feigen and Adam Glickman fell on the cutting room floor due to time limitations. "One of my favorites made it in for just a moment," says Wiltshire. "I trained Ernie, a Clydesdale, to piaffe—which is a dressage term in the equestrian world for running in place. I taught him to tap his feet on a board. Once he got the beat, he was into it. We played some Chuck Mangione for him and he didn't seem bothered when we added water falling down."

An entertaining behind-the-scenes video is available on the Wiltshires' website: www.turtleranch.net.

CHAPTER 3

Breeding and Training

The happiest times at the four Budweiser Clydesdale Breeding and Training Ranches are in the early spring, when mares give birth after eleven months of pregnancy. When born, the foals average three and one half feet tall at the withers, and weigh 125 pounds. (At maturity, they will stand six feet tall at the withers and weigh 2,000 pounds.) At the end of the pregnancy, the excellent health of the mares makes for generally speedy, painless deliveries.

Even so, the birthing process is always overseen by a veterinarian or trainer, who monitors both mother and foal. Because the horses are so large, multiple births are rare. The foals are sufficiently developed at birth to be able to stand, walk, and follow their mothers only a few hours after birth.

The foals spend their first six months at their mothers' sides nursing. During that period, mares are very attentive to their young and whinny if separated from them. After that time, the foals are weaned away with a mixture of feed and other nutrients. At the same time, they develop strength and independence and run in the pastures, either as a group or by themselves.

Dr. Dallas Goble, DVM, DACVS oversees the healthcare program for all of the Budweiser Clydesdales. He sees each horse at least once a year. Meticulous records are kept on the health histories of each of his "patients." Having accurate time series records on each of the Clydesdales is important. "We're able to make many health care decisions based on retrieved information," he says.

Goble times his visits to see the brood mares when the foals are born or are weaning. He also travels the country to examine the stallions and hitch members as well. "I do a complete physical on each horse annually." Like a personal trainer, Goble includes a nutritional evaluation, which is specific to each individual horse. "If any of the Budweiser Clydesdales is getting overweight," Goble declares, "we'll adjust his diet and his exercise program."

Goble praises the professionalism of the Clydesdale Operations staff. "The high level of expertise and dedication of the people on the ranches and with the hitches makes my job easy," he says. "The people who are responsible for the horses on a daily basis do a superb job. Today, we have such excellent care of the Clydesdales that essentially we don't have any problems at all."

Goble works closely with hitch supervisors and farriers to assure there is no stress on the horses as they travel. With Goble's consultation, the new horse trailers are designed with air suspension and padded floors to cushion their legs and feet. "Some of the Clydesdales, if you leave them at home, they just want to hop on the truck rather than get left behind." Goble is frequently on the telephone with the managers of the Clydesdale stables and hamlets.

The earliest harness
(identified as Chaldean)
was an inefficient
throat-girth harness
in the 3rd millennium BC.
The harder the horse
pulled, the more he was
choked. Naturally, the
farmers preferred oxen.
A somewhat more
modern breast-strap
harness was depicted
in scenes from
481 to 221 BC in China.
The precursor of the
modern collar harness
seems to have developed
in China, too—perhaps
as early as 477-499 AD.
This innovation did not
reach Europe until the
9th century AD, but it
made possible much more
efficient farming by horses.

From the earliest moments of life, the Budweiser Clydesdales are surrounded by loving, nurturing human beings who groom them, scratch their ears, play with them, feed them, and become their trusted friends. Combined with their naturally calm nature, this hands-on care makes these huge horses exceptionally easy to manage. In fact, this development of "ground manners" is the rudimentary first training for all horses.

Within days of their birth, foals will don their first light halter—usually cloth rather than leather. Weeks later, trainers will begin to lead the foal by the halter and eventually to attach the foal to tie-downs for grooming. Some horses are naturally accepting of their trainers' actions; others may jerk their heads at the halter or nip and kick before they learn to stand still.

Consistency and patient repetition by the trainers are key to the relationship, both now and from this point forward. Gradually, the daily interactions between trainers and Clydesdale foals create a respect and a trust for human beings that will last a lifetime for the horse. This is a trust that is never, ever violated—the Clydesdales are trained by positive reinforcement and never handled roughly or struck with rope or whip. Their early training is a system of responsibility and mutual understanding that becomes ever more important as they continue on their journey to the Budweiser Clydesdale hitch.

Jake, the two-year-old
shown here, is pulling
a sled in tandem
with an older horse.
He responds well
to trainer John Detweiler,
who is in charge of
training at Grant's Farm.
Jake pulls the sled
evenly and comfortably
at varied speeds, and
he makes efficient turns
on the grass.

At age two, Clydesdales are deemed mature enough to begin training for the hitch. The first relevant experience is wearing a bridle and being directed with reins. Ideally, the bit in the horse's mouth is used to communicate signals from the driver through the reins. The Clydesdales are well-trained to respond to the most subtle changes in pressure from the driver. The Clydesdale drivers know that gentle handling of the reins and the bit are completely effective under ordinary conditions. In emergency circumstances, however, the snaffle check bits go a long way toward bringing eight tons of horses—and a beer wagon—to a stop.

Once a two-year-old has become accustomed to the bridle and reins, he is fitted with a hitch harness—at first without the traces. Many young horses at this stage will buck and kick in an effort to throw off the harness, but eventually they settle down. Adding the traces may cause them to become tangled up, but in time they learn that if they stand quietly, the traces will not give them any trouble.

For most Clydesdales, the first experience of pulling a load is the training sled. This is a simple platform that slides along on rails rather than wheels. When pulled on grass, it has less drag than on sand, which gives the younger horse an opportunity to adjust to the feeling of pulling a rig.

Jake works one-on-one with trainer John Detweiler. This is Jake's opportunity to learn signals and commands he will need in the hitch, without being "coached" by an older horse.

This training cart is a contemporary version of what was known in the 19th century as a one-horse shay. The carriage was commonly used for errands about town, and could carry one or two people. The tradition of the horse-drawn cart or carriage goes all the way back to ancient Rome, where horses were used in everyday transportation, farming, mail delivery, and battle.

Only very wealthy Romans, however, had their own private horse-drawn carriages. What became known as the Carriage Era began in Europe in the 17th century, and crossed the Atlantic with the Pilgrims. It lasted into the early 20th century, until Henry Ford's Model T made the automobile affordable for the common man.

Pulling a light one-horse carriage is hardly any effort at all for a Clydesdale, who can comfortably pull a two-ton load–approximately twice his own weight. These pictures hark back to the horse-and-buggy era of America, when many families had their own rigs or buckboards for personal transportation, as well as for hauling goods to and from the market. At the turn of the last century, urban folks rode one of the many horse-drawn trolleys in the streets of every American city.

Jake seems to take a special pride in pulling this carriage, as if he knows that his efforts are taking him closer to the Budweiser hitch.

The brake pedal allows the driver to signal stops and turns to the team. It is also a rarely used safety mechanism for the driver to stop a headstrong horse.

The footboard separates the carriage from the horses and provides a sturdy platform for braking.

The fifth wheel, as this platform is called, allows the hitch to make tight maneuvers, including turning a complete circle.

The eveners connect the carriage to the horses' harnesses and are the mechanism by which the horses pull the carriage.

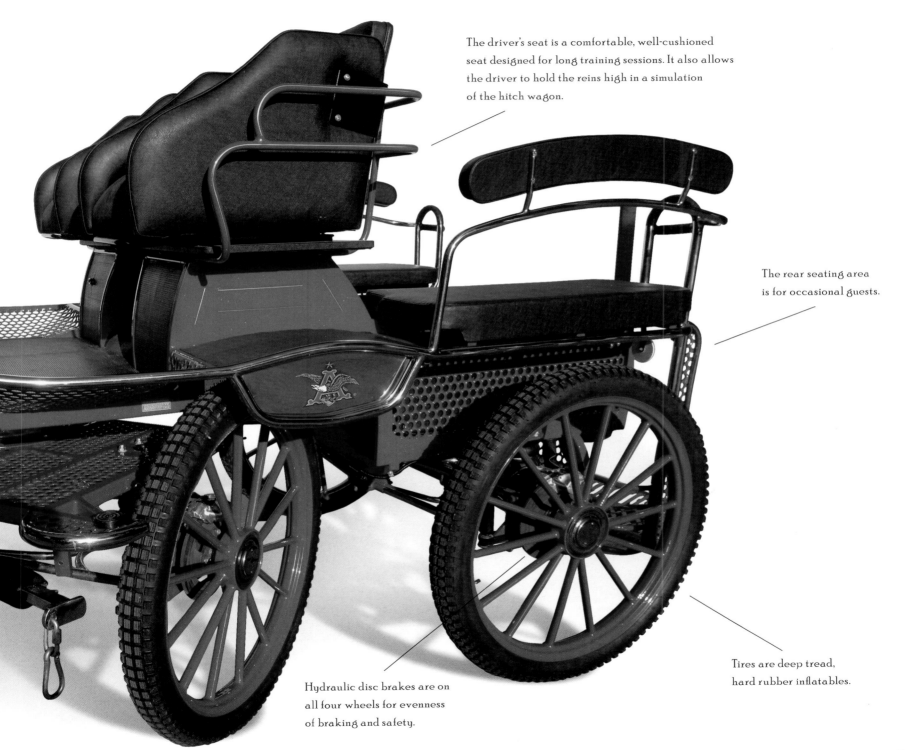

The driver's seat is a comfortable, well-cushioned seat designed for long training sessions. It also allows the driver to hold the reins high in a simulation of the hitch wagon.

The rear seating area is for occasional guests.

Hydraulic disc brakes are on all four wheels for evenness of braking and safety.

Tires are deep tread, hard rubber inflatables.

How do you train animals with heightened fright responses to be fearless in the face of honking automobile horns, noisy cheering crowds, police sirens, and even fireworks? There are three aspects to making a horse comfortable in an urban environment. First, the naturally calm and docile disposition of the Clydesdale anchors him in most situations; no doubt, his large size helps, too. Second, experience is a great teacher, and so are experienced horses. "The more miles you put on a horse," explains trainer Robin Wiltshire, "the more stable he becomes." From the time he begins his training, the hitch novice is partnered with an older, more experienced horse. If his partner is calm, chances are he will be, too. Most important of all is the confidence the horses develop in their relationships with handlers. They trust that their human friends will protect them, and the horses take their cues from them.

As driver and West Coast hitch manager Lloyd Ferguson notes, the Clydesdales are unusual: "I've seen these horses on runways with jets, in big, surging crowds of people, and even on the side of active automobile race tracks. They are just unflappable."

At last, all the years of effort pay off, and the young trainee is deemed ready to meet the public. With a hearty horse laugh, the newest high-stepping lead horse proudly takes his hard-earned place at the front of the hitch.

The rotation of new Clydesdales into the hitch is carefully planned. As has been the case throughout most of his training, the new kid on the block is paired with a more experienced sidekick, and in unfamiliar situations he takes his cue from his older buddy. Only one or two novices are worked into the team for any given performance, so that the hitch is always comprised primarily of experienced horses, who are teaching while they are performing.

CHAPTER 4

Clydesdales at Home

"There is no good reason
why an animal as clean,
as orderly, and as free
from destructive

disposition as a horse
should not be housed
as comfortably and
with as much regard
for sightlines
as a human being."
~Adolphus Busch

There are approximately 250 Budweiser Clydesdales in ranches, stables, and hamlets all over the United States. There are nine stables and entertainment parks where the Clydesdales are "at home" and happy to greet their admirers. First and foremost are the famous St. Louis 1885 stables that are located on the grounds of the 100-acre brewery. The St. Louis hitch appears in parades locally for various celebratory occasions. Second, not far away in the outskirts of St. Louis, is

Grant's Farm, where a Clydesdale Breeding and Training Ranch is open to the public at specific times. Here, you can often see mares with their foals and young horses being trained in skills to be used for parades and performances with the hitch.

In 1972, the Clydesdale Hamlet in Merrimack, New Hampshire was opened close to the brewery in the picturesque setting of the Merrimack Valley. Modeled after the Bauernhof at Grant's Farm, this area is included on tours of the brewery. Designed like a 19th century German farm Bauernhof, the Anheuser-Busch facility at Merrimack, New Hampshire is home to the East Coast

hitch of Budweiser Clydesdales. As a breeding facility, there are always horses in residence, even when the hitch is parading or performing. The Bauernhof consists of three components: stables for the horses, living quarters for the trainers and handlers, and a carriage house where beer delivery wagons, a Conestoga wagon, and a Concord coach are all on display.

The stable at the left
is located at SeaWorld
in San Diego, and the
Clydesdales on the right
welcome visitors to
the Clydesdale Hamlet
at SeaWorld, San Antonio.

Fort Collins, Colorado began as a frontier trading post in the shadow of 14,255-foot Longs Peak in the Rocky Mountains. Since then it has grown into a charming collegiate town, home of

Colorado State University. It is also the site of one of the twelve domestic Anheuser-Busch breweries, and a Clydesdale Hamlet.

There are five other locations where the Clydesdales receive visitors: the SeaWorlds in San Diego, California; Orlando, Florida; and San Antonio, Texas; as well as the Busch Gardens in Tampa Bay, Florida and Williamsburg, Virginia.

N
ewlyweds Ulysses S. Grant and Julia Dent Grant received the gift of 80 acres of farmland from the Dent family when they married in 1848. Located near St. Louis, it became known as Grant's Farm. The two-room log cabin farmhouse, hand-built by Grant himself, was aptly dubbed "Hardscrabble"—the farm was never an economic success. After Grant's death, the cabin was moved off the property to a site in Webster Groves, and was later put on display by the Blanke Coffee Company at the 1904 St. Louis World's Fair (properly

called the Louisiana Purchase Exposition). By this time, Adolphus Busch had acquired acreage that included the original Grant family homestead. After the fair closed, he purchased Hardscrabble and returned it to the property. August A. Busch, Sr. built his own elegant home at Grant's Farm, and used it to house his collection of farm and exotic animals. In addition to being the breeding home of the Clydesdales, today Grant's Farm is still home to elephants, buffalo, camels, donkeys, peacocks, and goats, and is open to the public.

At SeaWorld Orlando some huge mammals meet. Next to Shamu, even a Clydesdale looks a little smaller!

At the various SeaWorld and Busch Gardens theme parks around the country, the Budweiser Clydesdales are only one of many attractions. Nevertheless, the Clydesdale Hamlets are a popular destination, and the Clydesdales often participate in celebrations and parades around the parks.

Even underwater, the orcas feel the vibrations of the Budweiser Clydesdales as they come thundering along the road near the orcas' pools. Chuck Tompkins, the Corporate Curator of Zoological Operations at Busch Entertainment, says, "The whales are very fascinated with the sound and the visuals of the Clydesdales. They hear the hitch coming and jump up to see them as they pass by."

The Clydesdales will soon have another home. Scheduled for completion in 2008, a new 340-acre Clydesdale breeding and training facility is under construction in Cooper County, Missouri.

CHAPTER 5

The Natural Clydesdale

One of the most inspiring sights in nature is a horse running free, expressing a joy and sense of freedom that we recognize instantly.

The remarkable anonymous poem, which begins on the following page, perfectly describes the qualities of the magnificent Clydesdale horse:

Thudding hoof and flowing hair,
Style and action sweet and fair,
Bone and sinew well defined,
Movement close both fore and hind,

Noble eye and handsome head,
Bold, intelligent, well-bred,
Lovely neck and shoulder laid,
See how shapely he is made,

Muscle strong and frame well knit,
Strength personified and fit,
Thus the Clydesdale—see him go,
To the field, the stud, the show,

Proper back and ribs well sprung,
Sound of limb, and sound of lung,
Powerful loin, and quarter wide,
Grace and majesty allied,

Basic power–living force–the
Equine king–the Clydesdale horse.

CHAPTER 6

Clydesdales
Across America

It began with a simple idea: a plan to say "thank you" to the men and women serving in our armed forces around the globe. The sea-to-shining-sea logistics of carrying it through to completion, however, were a great deal more complicated.

The Clydesdales Across America: Here's to the Heroes tour was launched on April 22, 2005, when two Clydesdale hitches, one

starting from New York's 59th Street Bridge and one beginning on San Francisco's Golden Gate, left their respective coasts and headed for a rendezvous in the American heartland. Before they met up for a festive fireworks party on the 3rd of July, they had traveled more than 17,600 miles, visiting 21 cities in ten weeks.

Men and women from every branch of the American armed services participated in the Across America program.

A t each stop, people of all ages and walks of life turned out to see the Clydesdales, and to record messages of gratitude to those serving in the military. More than 13,000 greetings were gathered in all; they were broadcast throughout the rest of the year on the American Forces Radio and Television Service (AFRTS).

As part of the program, Anheuser-Busch sponsored free admission to Busch Gardens and SeaWorld theme parks to members of the armed forces for all of 2005. The offer was extended through 2008; eventually more than 4 million servicemen and women and their families took advantage of the opportunity.

"We hope this salute serves as a small token of our heartfelt appreciation to our nation's military for all the sacrifices they and their families make on a daily basis," said August Busch IV,

when the program began. "It's important for our military to know they have our nation's support. They fight for the freedom we enjoy every day, and we should never take that freedom or our American way of life for granted."

The Clydesdales headed for an unprecedented nose-to-nose meeting at mid-span on St. Louis' historic Eads Bridge, high above the Mississippi River. Along the way, the hitches stopped at cities and towns both large and small, appearing at Major League baseball games, local parades, festivals, and rodeos.

Rocky Sickmann, Director of Military Sales for Anheuser-Busch, coordinated the event with the Switch and Waylon agencies. "We felt it was important for American companies and everyday Americans to step up and let the troops know we support them," he said. "We had soccer teams, baseball teams, scouts, mothers, fathers, spouses, and families of active duty servicemen and women, firemen, policemen, mayors and senators, and celebrities like comedian Tom Arnold and Chipper Jones of the Atlanta Braves. Everyone delivered heartfelt and energetic messages. A 53-foot long mobile television recording studio traveled with each Clydesdale caravan; at every stop, family, friends, and everyday citizens recorded their thanks to our men and women overseas.

Tom Shipley, Director of Budweiser Marketing (pictured in the left-hand corner of the facing page) greeted the crowds at many Across America locations, and reminded them that all armed forces families were invited to enjoy free admission at all of the SeaWorlds and Busch Gardens, compliments of Anheuser-Busch.

The wishes of thousands of supporters from the Across America sites were played on American Forces Radio and Television Service (AFRTS) at military outposts in more than 177 countries worldwide. In addition, personal messages of thanks from troops overseas to supporters at home were met with enthusiasm and emotion as they played on two large screens in the mobile unit.

The Clydesdales were there for families to enjoy, but they also served as giant billboards to draw people to the program. "We had firefighters who had been involved in 9-11, and they were just driving down the road in their fire truck," recalls Sickmann. "They saw the Clydesdales and pulled over to send a message to the troops overseas. Police officers came by all day long, wherever we set up."

S ickmann was moved by the emotional impact of the program, both on those sending messages, and those receiving them. "It was especially gratifying to see so many people recording messages with their children. You could hear parents explaining what was going on to their kids," Sickmann continues. "They told them, 'The reason we're here is because of these people who are helping to protect us and care for us.' Some had popcorn or cotton candy when they were shooting their messages, and the parents told them, 'Hey! We're enjoying this day because somebody is providing us this freedom.' It was a great way to help educate the younger generation."

As a former Marine and Iran POW, Sickmann learned firsthand the value of a meaningful communications lifeline to friends and family back in the States.

"I was honored that they asked me to do this," he says. "It meant a lot to me, because I know how lonely those troops are far from home and in harm's way. It's not easy being here at home, either. Their families have to live and breathe their worry and their concern for their loved ones 24/7, even as they must continue to go about their daily lives. It's incredibly difficult."

125

Anheuser-Busch military veterans unfurled an 82-foot by 40-foot American flag from the side of the bridge. More than 336,000 watts of lights beamed 120,000 miles into space as the two teams of Clydesdales met atop the Eads Bridge at what was supposed to have been the end of their cross-country journey.

As it turned out, however, the Clydesdale odyssey wasn't over yet. Due to overwhelming public and military response, the Clydesdales Across America tour was extended—twice. The hitches and their mobile recording studios went on to several other cities and towns, including Milwaukee, Sturgis and Las Vegas before ending their tour in Philadelphia  in early December at the annual Army-Navy football game. By that time, the hitches had logged over 30,000 miles.

The tour came to a grand climax on July 3 in St. Louis. "The Here's to the Heroes Tour enjoyed great success in conveying the well wishes of thousands of Americans to the men and women of the U.S. military around the world," said Tom Shipley, Budweiser brand manager. "Hosting the nation's largest Independence Day celebration light show created the perfect finale to the Heroes Tour, and allowed us to share the moment with our fellow St. Louisians."

CHAPTER 7

A Clydesdale's Best Friend

Dalmatians are pure white at birth; an average of eight puppies are born in each litter. The puppies develop their first spots within the first week of life, and continue to develop additional spots into adulthood—and even into old age. Dalmatians have spots all over their bodies, not just on their coats but on the bottoms of their paws and on their tongues as well. When full grown they range from 19 to 24 inches in height, and weigh 40 to 70 pounds.

Dalmatians come from an ancient lineage. It is believed that they are the very first type of dog bred by people for specific desirable traits. Despite their name, however, it is doubtful that they originated in the Adriatic province of Dalmatia. There are Egyptian tomb paintings of Dalmatian ancestors running with chariots; a 14th century fresco in Florence's Santa Maria Novella basilica depicts several Dalmatian forebears in the company of Dominican friars. The first reference to the Dalmatian as a breed occurs in 18th century manuscripts.

George Washington and Benjamin Franklin were Dalmatian owners for the same reason as many other well-bred 18th century gentlemen. Dalmatians first came to prominence in the era of elegant horse-drawn carriages, which were the main mode of genteel transportation from the 17th through the 19th centuries. They were known as the "English coach dog" or the "carriage dog."

Dalmatians were historically bred for their endurance. They had the speed and the stamina to keep up with a team of carriage horses, even over a day's journey of 20 to 30 miles. Running with the horses was a joyous way for them to get the exercise they need.

In the late 19th century the sleek spotted dogs continued in this role, but with the opening of the American West, they began to accompany stagecoaches as well. Lawlessness on the frontier was common, and horses–then as now–were valuable animals. To protect their four-legged assets from horse thieves, stage drivers would sling a hammock between two stalls and hope to get some sleep while on guard. Soon, however, it became clear that these fearless and intelligent dogs had bonded with the horses, and would protect them from intruders. As a result, the men developed enough confidence in their Dalmatians to take overnight lodgings in the roadhouses that sprang up along the major stage routes.

Samuel Edmund Waller's "Home from the Honeymoon" captures two fashionable newlyweds and their stylish carriage.

It was
Benjamin Franklin
who introduced
Dalmatians into
America's newly
created volunteer
firehouses. As they had
with elegant carriages,
they would often run
ahead of the horses,
barking and clearing
the streets. When the
rigs arrived at a fire,
the dogs would guide
the horses to safe areas
away from the flames
and protect them
from theft, and even
from other dogs.

From their role as carriage dogs and stagecoach companions, it was a small step to their new position with America's volunteer firefighters. Dalmatians, with their heightened guarding instinct, their strong athletic build, and their affinity for horses, were a natural addition to firehouses across the country. They are also very loyal to their human companions. Although horses in general are quite fearful of fire, they had to be willing to bring the firemen and their equipment as close to the flames as possible. Once on the scene, the Dalmatians made sure nothing was stolen from the fire apparatus.

As the combustion engine replaced horse-drawn fire equipment, the Dalmatians stayed in the firehouses. They had proven to be good companions not just for the horses, but for the firemen as well. There are numerous stories of heroic rescues and acts of bravery by the firehouse dogs, and even more stories of man-and-dog friendships. Firehouse lore perpetuated the mythology that the dogs gained a spot for each fire on which they worked.

Taken in 1942, this photo captures both the majesty of the breed
and his sense of belonging in the company of man.

The Dalmatians who travel with the Clydesdales made their official debut on March 30, 1950, at the groundbreaking ceremony for the Newark Brewery. Two weeks later they were seen for the first time by a much larger segment of the public. The Clydesdale hitch, with Dalmatian, starred in the opening credits for a new TV variety program called *The Ken Murray Show,* which premiered in 1950 on CBS and was sponsored by Anheuser-Busch.

They've been a fixture with the Clydesdales ever since. Simply put, the Dalmatians and the hitches are a great fit. The Dalmatians bonded right away with the Clydesdales, as they had with the carriage horses and the fire horses. Surrounded by the drivers and crew who travel with the Clydesdales, the Dalmatians also have plenty of human companionship. Living and traveling with them make it easy for the energetic dogs to get the vigorous daily exercise they need, and the dogs protect the horses from strangers.

"There really is an historical reason why we chose Dalmatians," says Jim Poole, Director of Clydesdale Operations for Anheuser-Busch. "In the early days of brewing, Dalmatians were bred and trained to protect the horses and guard the wagon when the driver went inside to make deliveries. The black-and-white spotted dogs were swift enough to keep up with the wagons, and their light-colored bodies and markings made them easier for both the drivers and horses to see during the twilight hours."

There is quite a bit of showmanship in the Dalmatians. Like their equine pals, they thrive on the attention they receive; they look good, and they know it. Although all Clydesdale hitch members are geldings, the Dalmatians who travel with them can be either male or female. Also like the horses, they are brushed and groomed before each performance to keep them looking their best. Unlike many breeds that shed seasonally, Dalmatians shed continuously, and their barbed hairs seem to work their way into whatever fabric they touch.

Dalmatians apprentice with the hitches the same way that the horses do. When a veteran dog is nearing retirement, he is tethered to his replacement, so the new kid on the block learns the ropes from the old pro.

The wagon that the Clydesdales pull is quite tall; the drivers sit 10 feet off the ground, too far for a Dalmatian to safely get on or off without assistance. Before every performance, a crew member lifts the Dalmatian onto the wagon, then ties his harness to the seat for his (or her) own protection.

Once on board, there is a look on the faces of these dogs as they sit high up on the wagon with the drivers and listen to the applause of the crowds. They know that they are something special.

This 2005 spot, *Separated at Birth*, proves that although getting chosen as a firehouse dog is cool, there are other fates which are cooler–much cooler. When we first meet the Dalmatian pups, they are littermates sharing the same basket. They are both adorable, but one catches the eyes of the firemen at the stationhouse and is chosen as their mascot. The second is left to an uncertain fate, which

Ad Agency: DDB Chicago; Creative Team: Craig Feigen, Adam Glickman, Greg Popp, Don Pogany; Director: Buddy Cohen

is finally revealed when the fire truck draws up next to a Budweiser Clydesdale hitch. In this ultimate game of sibling one-upmanship, the firehouse mascot suddenly realizes that he is only second best. The Dalmatians take neener-neener to new heights as the final canine raspberry from the Clydesdale hitch Dalmatian brings a soft but anguished howl of remorse from the retreating fire truck.

CHAPTER 8

The Beauty Treatment

Each day,
a 2,000-pound horse
consumes 20 to 25 quarts
of crimped oats,
bran, dried beet pulp,
molasses, salt
and hot water,
often with vitamins
and minerals added.
He will eat
a 50-pound bale
of timothy hay
and drink approximately
30 gallons of water daily.
On extremely hot
summer days,
water consumption
can be as high
as 60 gallons.

The Budweiser Clydesdales look great every time they appear in public. That's because, unlike supermodels or movie stars who only dress for the runway or the red carpet, these horses are given the beauty treatment each day. We're not talking about a couple of hours at the beauty salon each week for a haircut, facial, manicure, and pedicure. This is a daily routine requiring five to six hours, six handlers, and a whole lot of attention to detail. On performance days, the horses spend an additional 45 minutes each getting "dressed" in the elaborate, custom-fitted harnesses that they wear in the hitch.

Thorough grooming is not entirely a matter of beauty. Each time a handler washes and brushes a horse, he or she is also massaging the animal. (Much like humans, Clydesdales generally enjoy the grooming treatment.) It is an opportunity for the handler to carefully inspect the horse and feel for any unusual lumps or cuts. Naturally, grooming is also essential to good health. A clean and well groomed horse has less chance of developing rashes or infections in his surprisingly delicate skin. And by curry combing or brushing the horse, the handler stimulates natural oils that give his coat a special luster.

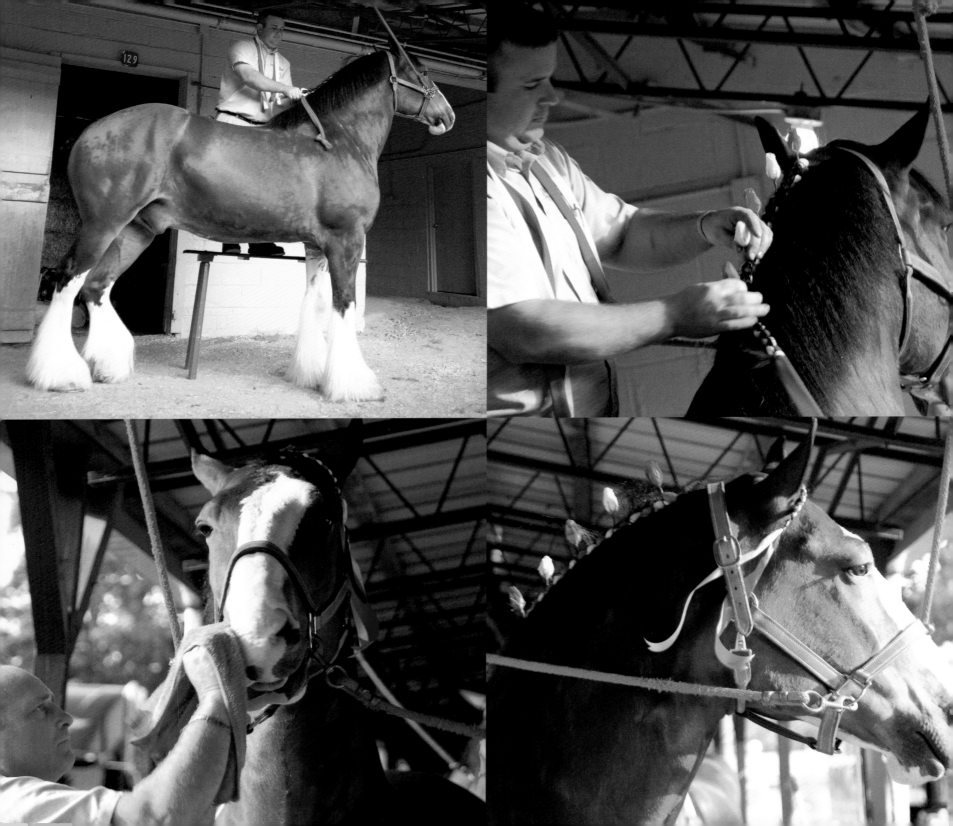

The sun has not arisen some mornings when the Clydesdales begin to prepare for a 10:00 am performance. For the most part, the horses lie down to sleep at night, which is undoubtedly more restful for their hardworking legs. As their handlers come by to offer a breakfast bite, they arise and whinny in anticipation of a "miracle morning" and a parade day. After eating, each horse is hosed down with a shower of warm water and quickly toweled dry. (The Clydesdales

are periodically body-washed with gentle soap without chemicals which might irritate or dry out their skin.)

A handler then begins the process of curry combing and brushing the entire massive body. The curry comb is a typically oval tool with plastic or rubber teeth that massages deep in the horse's coat and brings up dirt and loose hair. Usually, the handler works with a body brush in the opposite hand and sweeps over the area that just has been curry combed. He brushes with the direction of the horse's hair to smooth it down, stopping periodically to clean both the curry comb and the brush. This process begins at the head and neck and finishes with the hindquarters. The horses seem particularly to enjoy this part of their daily routine. They lean into the handler's efforts and move to help him or her with the ministrations.

One part of the Clydesdale that is shampooed every day is the feathers on each leg. These distinctive fluffs of long, snow-white hair that grow over each hoof are an identifying element of the breed. Because the horse's natural gait causes him to lift his feet like a high stepper as he walks, the feathers are especially important to the Budweiser hitches. They emphasize the movement and add to the drama of the hitch as it passes in parade.

Their proximity to the ground means that the feathers easily collect mud or dirt. They are shampooed daily with Castile, or vegetable-based, soap. (In the process of shampooing the feathers, the handler also runs his or her hands over each leg of the horse and checks for any problems or areas of irritation.) To enhance the natural whiteness of the hair, the handlers may add a natural brightener known as flowers of sulphur. After thorough rinsing, the feathers are carefully dried. They are then sprayed with a special solution of oils, both to replace any natural oils that were shampooed away, and to keep the hairs soft and supple.

From the very beginning of the Budweiser Clydesdale hitch, the horses' manes and tails were beautifully braided with ribbons and paper flowers. The braiding is both attractive and functional. Because free tail hairs could easily become tangled in the reins or harness, the braiding is an important safety measure.

Celebrated photographer Margaret Bourke-White captured this image of the braiding process in 1954, and the process remains the same today.

Starting at the top of the neck, the handler begins wrapping a red and a white strand of ribbon (each about forty inches) through the mane, holding tufts of hair together tightly. This is repeated many times until the entire mane is braided. Then, red and white paper roses are attached by the wire stems to the braided mane at approximately four-inch intervals.

To braid the tail, the hairs are carefully combed out and separated into three strands. These are then interwoven with ribbons. The braided tail is then wrapped up in a ball, which is tied tightly with string. Finally, a decorative bow is tied around the ball.

"Everything about the Clydesdales is special—including their feet," says master farrier Tim Kriz, who travels around the country shoeing and re-shoeing the East Coast Clydesdale hitches as they travel. "First, their feet—or hooves—are simply much bigger than the average horse and they are carrying much more weight on those hooves. Second, the hooves and legs of these horses take an unusual pounding because of all the parade work they do on hard surfaces."

As Kriz points out, simply fitting a horseshoe to a Clydesdale's hoof is a larger job than usual, in every sense of the word. The Clydesdale hoof is bigger, heavier, and subject to many different kinds of stress.

Making one Clydesdale shoe can often require more than an hour of hot, muscle-straining work at the forge. The hoof is first trimmed of excess growth—pretty much the way you would

trim a toenail. Because the Budweiser Clydesdales wear horseshoes that are five times the weight of the ordinary horseshoe, they are custom-designed to protect the horse's hoof and give the horse good footing on hard surfaces.

"One of the most important parts of a farrier's work is examining the hooves for problems or diseases. 'Splitting' can be a particularly difficult and sometimes painful problem for a horse. We really have to know as much about horses' hooves as most veterinarians. Each time I shoe a Clydesdale, I look carefully at each hoof for problems. Of course, it takes years of experience and observation to learn."

Tim Kriz ought to know. He's the third generation of farriers who have hammered out the shoes for the Budweiser Clydesdales. He is actually the eighth generation of farriers in his family—and is hoping that his son will be the ninth!

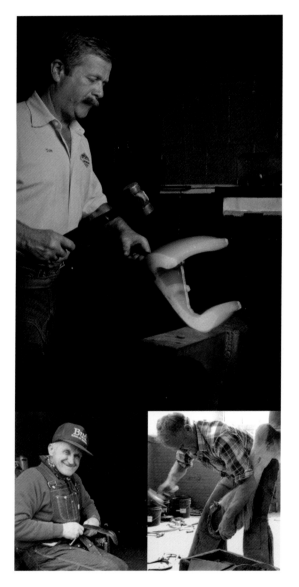

Joseph Kriz, Sr., Tim's grandfather, was a sixth generation farrier who came to the United States from his native Prague, Czechoslovakia in the 1920s. He opened a blacksmith shop in Bethany, Connecticut, and was eventually joined by his sons and his grandsons. The fact that tractors had begun to replace horses didn't bother him. Kriz traveled to the Midwest, where he bought many Belgians, Percherons, and Clydesdales, later to resell them in New England. Before long, he became known throughout the region as the best source for draft horses–and their shoes.

Today, the Kriz family has a 30-acre ranch with horses, cattle, dogs, a donkey, and lots of wild geese nearby. From that headquarters, Tim and his brother Glenn take care of the Clydesdale hitches based in the East and Midwest, including St. Louis. Sometimes, the Merrimack hitch even comes to them when they are on the road. Several of the hitch drivers fondly recall staying with the Kriz family en route to the Macy's Thanksgiving Day Parade in New York. Tim recalls that his mother used to cook three or four large turkeys to feed as many as 250 guests who would come to celebrate with them and the Clydesdales.

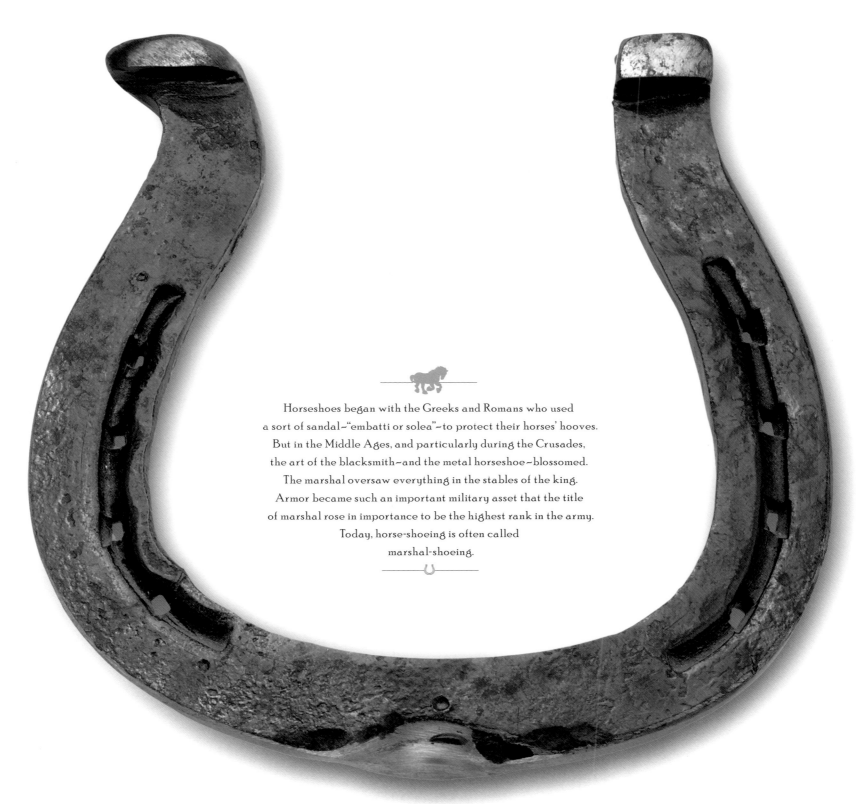

Horseshoes began with the Greeks and Romans who used
a sort of sandal~"embatti or solea"~to protect their horses' hooves.
But in the Middle Ages, and particularly during the Crusades,
the art of the blacksmith~and the metal horseshoe~blossomed.
The marshal oversaw everything in the stables of the king.
Armor became such an important military asset that the title
of marshal rose in importance to be the highest rank in the army.
Today, horse-shoeing is often called
marshal-shoeing.

The elaborate harness worn by the Budweiser Clydesdale hitches is a beautiful and expensive piece of custom design. Created by the late John Santos of Great Barrington, Massachusetts, each harness is handcrafted from brass and leather, and weighs 130 pounds. The stitching requires pure linen thread, and several different kinds of leather are used in the unique design.

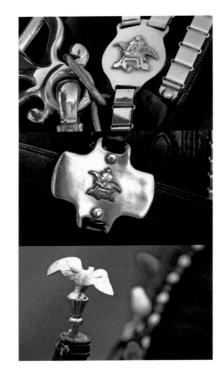

Fashionistas may find haute couture designs by Balenciaga, Chanel, or Christian Dior to be pricey, but what the Clydesdales wear is truly "oat couture." Like haute couture, each harness and collar is custom-fitted to its individual wearer. Two handlers clean and polish the leather and brightwork of each harness daily, and make certain that every element is in good repair.

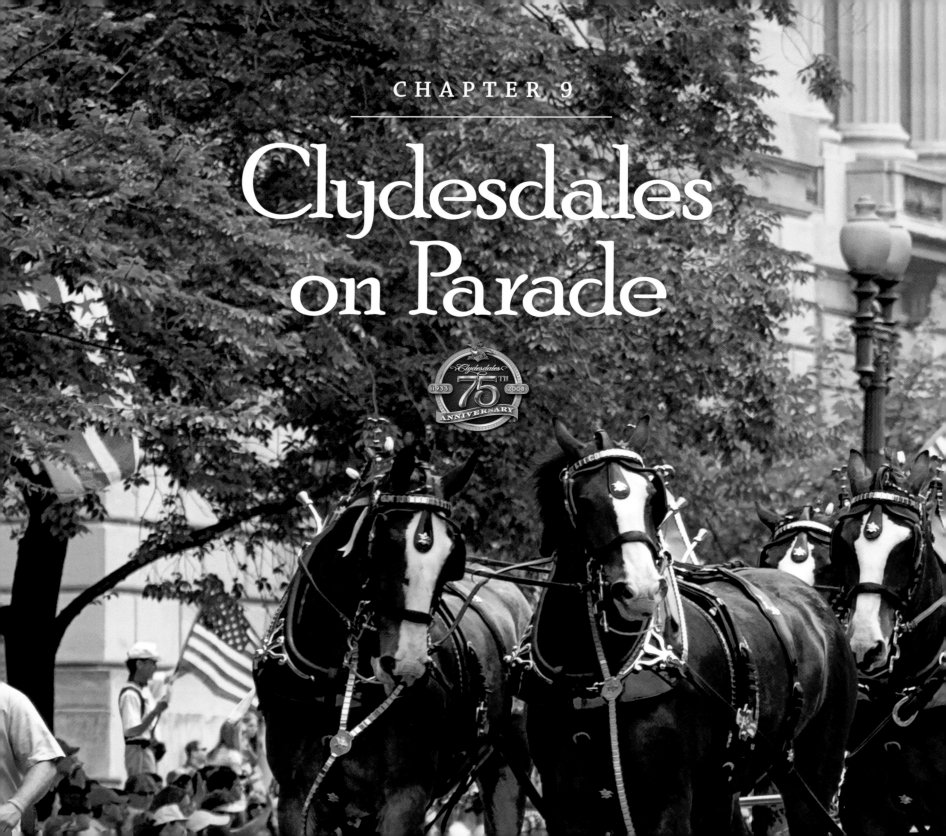

CHAPTER 9

Clydesdales
on Parade

Five hitches travel well over 100,000 miles combined every year to bring the Budweiser Clydesdales to parades, fairs, and exhibitions all over the United States. The hitches with home bases in St. Louis, Missouri; Menifee, California; and Merrimack, New Hampshire will travel about 300 days a year each. The two hitches from San Diego, California and San Antonio, Texas travel from their home bases about half that amount of time. Still, of the more than 1,000 requests and invitations for appearances that the Clydesdales receive each year, they are only able to handle less than half. Some of that is due to strict limitations on performance time (no longer than four hours in harness) and travel time (no more than 500 miles per day).

In addition to annual appearances at events such as the Rose Parade and the Los Angeles County Fair, schedulers make certain that the hitches also come to small towns in America; to hospitals, senior centers, and veterans' gatherings.

The Clydesdales have traveled in style ever since their beginnings in 1933, when the hitch moved from city to city by railroad car. In 1940, a group of automotive vans were specially designed to transport the Budweiser Clydesdale hitch. The vans have been replaced regularly, and the new big rigs are shining examples of good quality air-conditioning, custom-designed suspension systems, and smooth rides. Every handler or driver who travels with the hitch must have a commercial driver's license.

Each hitch travels with three vans, two of which carry the Clydesdales (usually a total of 10, to give each member of the Budweiser hitch an opportunity to rest) and the third van is filled with the carriage, the harnesses, and the traveling stalls.

On a few rare occasions, the Clydesdales have flown via transport airplanes to appear internationally in Japan. The Budweiser Clydesdales have also flown to Puerto Rico and Alaska for appearances. The hitch has never been transported by boat.

Because the Budweiser Clydesdale teams frequently parade on asphalt or cement surfaces, and because they carry considerable harnesses in addition to their own weight, their feet and legs need special care. Their horseshoes are custom-fitted by a farrier (or blacksmith) every six weeks. Each shoe weighs about five pounds, which is five times as heavy as the horseshoe worn by a riding horse. The shoes are also implanted with borium studs for more secure footing on concrete surfaces. Each horseshoe is carefully nailed to

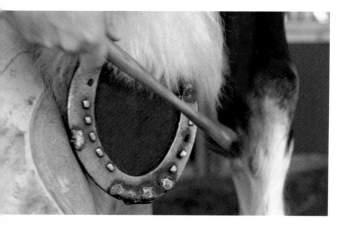

the hoof of the horse with eight number-twelve nails, which are each three inches long. The huge (nine inches in diameter) hooves of the Clydesdale are composed of keratin, a tough substance much like the material of a human fingernail, and have no nerves. Thus, the periodic cutting of the hooves and the shoeing are painless.

To protect the inner part of the Clydesdale's hoof (called the "frog") from damage or infection, a thick leather covering is inserted between the horseshoe and the hoof.

The Clydesdales come from a noble lineage: their ancestors were the Great Horses, ridden by knights in shining armor. Because of their size and strength, they gave their knights a distinct advantage on the battlefield. The breed emerged in Scotland in the 17th century, when one of the dukes of Hamilton imported some Belgian Great Horses and bred them with local mares. Clydesdales first came to the United States around the time of the Civil War as strong draft horses to pull wagons and plows.

One of the most requested appearance days for the Budweiser Clydesdales is one of the biggest national holidays, July 4th. Teams of photographers recorded the different ways that the Clydesdales participated in parades and celebrations in different parts of the country on July 4th From big metropolises, such as Chicago, IL and Washington, DC, to small towns, such as Rancho Cordova, CA, crowds were waving flags, downing hot dogs and corn-on-the-cob, and cheering for the Clydesdales. In addition to those cities and

towns, teams of photographers were stationed at Bonners Ferry, ID; Williamsburg, IA; and Lewisburg, PA. Rancho Cordova, for example, is a small city near Sacramento with 59,000 patriotic residents. Here, the Clydesdales paraded daily through Hagan Park from their temporary stables and viewing area. The park was set up with a carnival midway that featured rides for the children, lots of food for everyone, and plenty of fireworks. The Fourth of July Parade down Coloma Road was the highlight of the week-long festivities.

For 75 years, the Budweiser Clydesdales have participated in all kinds of American celebrations, especially parades. One of the most famous parades in America is the Mardi Gras parade in New Orleans. The Clydesdale hitch used to be famous for tossing silver doubloons from the wagon, which could be redeemed for free beers. (Many of the revelers preferred to hold onto them as keepsakes.) In 1953, they began a tradition of performing in the biggest parade of them all, the Tournament of Roses Parade in Pasadena, California. For many years, Mrs. Carlota ("Lotsie") Busch designed the floats for the city of St. Louis, and the floats have garnered more than their share of awards for beauty and innovation. In 1967, the Clydesdale hitch first appeared in the Macy's Thanksgiving Day parade in New York City. In fact, you name a sizeable city in the United States and it is almost certain that the Budweiser Clydesdales have paraded there regularly.

This commemorative poster celebrates the appearance of the Budweiser Clydesdales in a 1980s Cotton Bowl Parade.

The Clydesdales were there for opening day of the 2006 baseball season, helping inaugurate the new Busch Stadium in April, 2006. It proved to be a banner year for the St. Louis Cardinals, who were crowned World Series Champs that October. The Clydesdales led off the joyous celebration that followed, triumphantly delivering

the Commissioner's Trophy into Busch Stadium to the delight of wildly cheering fans. (In the photograph above, Cardinals manager, Tony LaRussa, catches the game ball delivered by the Budweiser Clydesdale hitch in St. Louis, on April 6, 2008. It proved to be good luck, because that day the Cardinals finished a three-game sweep of the Washington Nationals.)

CHAPTER 10

Clydesdales in the Holidays

There have been
numerous TV spots
celebrating the holidays.
For example,
the image on the left
of Lloyd Ferguson
and his assistant
driving a hitch
through picturesque
Telluride, Colorado.
Telluride is fully
decked out
for the holidays;
the spot was shot on
November 25, 2002.

From the inception of the hitch in 1933 to the present, the Budweiser Clydesdales have been the goodwill ambassadors for Anheuser-Busch. As the enduring symbols of quality and tradition, they are beloved by generations of Americans. Never is this emotional connection more evident than during our most celebratory time of year, the holidays. From numerous Thanksgiving Day parades to that great kick-off of every new year, the Tournament of Roses Parade, Americans join with millions around the globe to enjoy the gentle beauty and majesty of the Clydesdales.

In December of 1976, Anheuser-Busch debuted its first television holiday spot. It was difficult to create because the winter of 1975–1976 was nearly snowless in New England. The Merrimack hitch waited for several months before the weather was ready. Finally, on March 15, 1976, the cameras rolled as the Clydesdales forged ahead into a blizzard that would eventually drop eleven inches of snow on the picture-perfect town of Woodstock, Vermont. (The handlers had been concerned that the horses would slip under snowy, icy conditions. As it turned out, however, the horses did fine; it was the wagon that kept slipping.)

When Anheuser-Busch sends out the Clydesdale card with its traditional greeting—"From Our Family to Yours"—it reflects the strong family ties that have characterized the brewery since the beginning. In almost every division of the company, employees who are the sons, daughters, nieces, nephews, grandsons and granddaughters of other longtime employees both past and present are a familiar sight. And since Adolphus Busch joined Eberhard Anheuser, his father-in-law, in the brewery in the 1860s, the leadership of the company has never been without a member of the Busch family at or near the helm.

As Anheuser-Busch Executive Vice-President Bob Lachky puts it: "Our evergreen holiday campaign is a way to say 'Happy Holidays' and to thank our friends and customers for their continued support."

These beautiful holiday cards have featured the Clydesdales since the early 1930s in a variety of ways. Many are scenes of a hitch galloping through the snow, often hauling a tree. Others are more playful fantasies of the Clydesdales pulling a sleigh through the skies. The card in the center of this page even shows the horses and a Dalmatian peering down a snow-capped chimney, as if puzzled as to what might be taking so long.

Each year the Anheuser-Busch Brewery in St. Louis is ablaze with holiday decorations. The 1885 stable is a special center of holiday celebration. In the picture above, the Clydesdales have their own special tree with presents and treats in holiday packages. This is a wonderful season for visitors and employees alike to enjoy the holidays.

Even for viewers in Hawaii and California, the ideal fantasy of the holidays is the snow-covered landscape of New England. This explains why so many of the pictures, such as the television spot of 1986, have been taken in places such as South Woodstock, Vermont. In the background is the Kedron Valley Inn which is celebrating its 185th anniversary.

Clydesdale memorabilia has always been a welcome holiday gift. And as the years have gone by, the many steins, trays, pillows and other keepsakes continue to evoke the quality and tradition of the Clydesdales. Pictured above are commemorative steins for the 2008 75th Anniversary. Below are Clydesdale collectible steins from previous years.

Acknowledgements

Thanks for the continued emphasis on quality and tradition in every aspect of Anheuser-Busch must go, first and foremost, to August A. Busch IV and his team of marketing executives at Anheuser-Busch, Inc., including Dave Peacock, Vice President Marketing; Evan Athanas, Vice President Sales; Keith Levy, Vice President Brand Management; Bob Lachky, Executive Vice President–Global Industry Development and Creative Development; Tony Ponturo, Vice President Global Media and Sports Marketing; Jim Sprick, Senior Director Special Services; and Marlene Coulis, Vice President Consumer Strategy and Innovation.

The Budweiser Brand Team, led by Dan McHugh, Director of Marketing for the Budweiser family of beers, deserves credit for managing Clydesdale marketing elements. Tom Shipley, Director Budweiser

Anheuser-Busch Clydesdale Operations Management
Standing: Dave Hennen, Dick Rosen, Robin McNabb, and Scott Smith.
Kneeling: Jim Poole with Doc, the Dalmatian

Marketing, leads the Budweiser Brand Team. Bob Fishbeck, Budweiser Product Manager, is the invaluable Anheuser-Busch Executive Producer of this book. (I would be remiss if I neglected to mention the numerous contributions of Elizabeth Jankowski, administrative assistant to Mr. Shipley and Mr. Fishbeck.) Denny Galati, Vice President Creative Development and Mary Hensley,

Manager Broadcast Production, play key advertising development roles. Randall Blackford, former Budweiser Marketing Director and Paul Simmons, Director Marketing–Northeast, initiated plans for this celebratory book.

The design and art direction team of Gary Alfredson, Creative Director, and Larry Butts, Associate Creative Director, at DDB Chicago, along with my wife and partner, Kay Diehl, have worked tirelessly and skillfully right along with me through the year-long process of creating this book. The result, of which I am most proud, is their baby as much as it is mine.

Marty Kohr, SVP and Group Business Director ,DDB Chicago, is the agency Executive Producer. More than a year ago, he brought this project opportunity to the attention of Steve Jackson, SVP and Worldwide Account Director. Working with Marty on production and all of the many details to make this book a reality were Heather Jensen, VP Executive Print Producer; Matt Davis, SVP Production Director; Mike Rostron, Senior Print Producer; Patty Phassos, Production Business Manager; JT Mapel, SVP Group Business Director; Jo Ann Reksel, Account Manager; Ryan Barrer, Account Manager; and Alison Whitelaw, Administrative Assistant.

Special acknowledgement goes to Bob Scarpelli, Chairman, Chief Executive Officer DDB Worldwide, who has helped to strengthen the Clydesdales for over 25 years.

On my first visit to St. Louis in August, 2007, I met with Anheuser-Busch Archivist Tracy Lauer, who loaded me with research, images, good advice and dinner on The Hill. She and her staff, including Lynn Fendler and Jeffrey Sahaida and Nelia Cromley, as well as Archivist Emeritus Bill Vollmar and Corporate Librarians Ann Lauenstein and Mary Butler are the keepers of the flame for Anheuser-Busch and provided invaluable historical materials for this book. Of course, the man who is Mr. Clydesdale and oversees every aspect of the lives of some 250 horses is the General Manager of Clydesdale Operations, Jim Poole, who has been unfailingly generous with his knowledge, time, and assistance. His staff—including the meticulous Robin McNabb, Division Secretary; Dave Hennen, Field Operations Manager; Scott Smith, Scheduling Supervisor, and Dick Rosen, Administrative Manager—gave me complete access and the benefit of their extensive experiences with these wonderful horses. Rocky Sickmann, Director of Military Sales, was an important source for the Clydesdales Across America chapter. Dan Hoffmann, Vice President Corporate Identity, was kind enough to explain the complex world of Anheuser-Busch products beyond beer. Dan Kopta, Manager of the Corporate Theater, helped us find images and information about the television spots. Bill Etling, Ellen Bogard and Brian Eaton of Anheuser-Busch Communications also provided access, background and assistance for many Clydesdale events.

There are many people beyond the immediate Anheuser-Busch, St. Louis/DDB Chicago family who have also contributed to the making of this book. I am especially grateful to John Detweiler, Supervisor of the Grant's Farm stables; Andy Elmore, Manager of Grant's Farm; John Soto, Supervisor of the Menifee, California stables, and Hans Jager, Supervisor of the Merrimack, New Hampshire stables, as well as West Coast hitch supervisor and dean of all hitch drivers Lloyd Ferguson; San Diego hitch drivers Kendra Lewkow and Lester Nisley; and Glenn Eickoff in Orlando. Robin Wiltshire and his wife, Kate–the extraordinary animal trainers for the famous Clydesdale commercials–regaled me with remarkable stories about the horses. Veterinarian to the Clydesdale stars is Dr. Dallas Goble, who travels around the country from his home in Tennessee, making sure that these are the healthiest horses in the nation. My friends and our publishing consultants, Rich Barber and Peter Berinstein, were engaged in every step of this enterprise. I am also grateful to other advertising agencies assisting Anheuser-Busch–including Waylon and Switch.

DDB's StudioChicago, which contributed so valuably to the production of this book, includes: Yvette Doud, Christina Guzy Kuhn, Annie Bandeko, Mike Johnson, Richard LaLiberte , Christopher Tuscan, Tom Waterloo, Joe Moreno, Ken Ejka and Marc Schwartzberg.

No doubt I have failed to acknowledge others who have made contributions, and I hope that they will forgive me. But finally, I want to give the biggest piece of credit to those beautiful, wordless horses who have given us all so much pleasure for 75 years, and will continue to do so long into the future: the amazing Budweiser Clydesdales.

Photography Credits

The majority of images in this book come from files in various Anheuser-Busch corporate divisions, particularly the Archives, Clydesdale Operations, and the Corporate Theater. However, Phil Schoulberg, the Anheuser-Busch official photographer, deserves special thanks for long hours shooting numerous images especially for this book. Special thanks, also, to Charlie Westerman and Richard Hamilton Smith, who are two top award-winning photographers who have chronicled the Clydesdales for decades. Bob Couey, Jason Collier, and Bob French were extraordinarily helpful in providing photographs from the Clydesdale hamlets around the country.

As members of the Across America team, for the Switch Agency, Craig Jakubs and Michael Strauss provided beautiful images. A special thanks to Dave and Barbara Hubert for the photo of their 1902 "American" Steam Fire Engine and Dalmatian named Blaze.

One of the best known contemporary artists, LeRoy Neiman, painted this portrait of a Budweiser Clydesdale and presented it to Anheuser-Busch, Inc., as a gift. This image of the painting appears on the endpapers with permission from Mr. Neiman.

Two photography researchers deserve credit for their exceptional efforts. Kay Diehl dug through eBay and numerous Internet sources to discover several early images of the Clydesdales that had been buried in the sands of time. Karen Blatchford, Senior Art Producer, DDB Chicago is the wizard of the stock photography houses, such as GettyImages and Corbis, and she found several important images hidden in their files. Karen also sent out a special team of photographers on the Fourth of July to capture the Clydesdales in action. The photographers, who came back with some excellent images of the Clydesdales, included: Karl Mondon in Rancho Cordova, CA; Aaron Frizzell in Bonners Ferry, ID; Mark Davitt in Williamsburg, IA; Jim Sloane in Washington, DC; Sean Simmers in Lewisburg, PA; and Steve Grubman in Chicago, IL.

I am also grateful to Kate Wiltshire for several "behind-the-scenes" images and to Norma Kriz for background and photographs of her remarkable multi-generational family of farriers to the Clydesdales. Thanks to the Pasadena Tournament of Roses for the historical Rose Parade images. Also thanks to the city of East Peoria, IL for an image from their Festival of Lights parade.